The Singing Sleuth Gets Snowed Under

The Singing Sleuth Gets Snowed Under

D.B. Barton

Usher Press

New York   Jacksonville

The Singing Sleuth Gets Snowed Under

by D.B. Barton

Copyright 2025
Cover by Barbara Lambros

This is a work of fiction. All the characters, names, incidents, and dialogue in this novel are either products of the author's imagination or are used fictitiously.

The Singing Sleuth Print Series:
The Singing Sleuth (2005, 2012)
The Singing Sleuth Returns (2007, 2014)
The Singing Sleuth Goes Home (2009, 2017)
The Singing Sleuth Crosses the Pond (2011, 2021)
The Singing Sleuth Does Vegas (2013)
The Singing Sleuth Takes a Bow (2016)
The Singing Sleuth Meets His Matches (2020)
The Singing Sleuth Runs a B&B (2022)
The Singing Sleuth Finds a Leaf (2023)
The Singing Sleuth Digs Up the Past (2024)
The Singing Sleuth Gets Snowed Under (2025)
The Singing Sleuth Sings On (2026)

The complete series can be ordered directly from
www.singingsleuth.com.

Printed in the United States of America

To those
who live to eat
and *not* eat to live.

You're not alone!

Contents

Pegasus Itinerary

Nine-Day Alaskan Cruise
Seattle to Seattle

Date	Day	Port of Call	Arrival	Departure
3-Aug	Sun	Seattle, Washington		3:00 PM
3-Aug	Sun	Pugent Sound *Scenic Cruising Only*		
4-Aug	Mon	*At Sea*		
5-Aug	Tue	Stephens Passage *Scenic Cruising Only*		
5-Aug	Tue	Juneau, Alaska	1:00 PM	9:00 PM
6-Aug	Wed	Endicott Arms/Dawes Glacier *Scenic Cruising Only*		
7-Aug	Thur	Sitka, Alaska	8:00 AM	4:00 PM
8-Aug	Fri	Ketchikan, Alaska	7:00 AM	6:00 PM
9-Aug	Sat	Prince Rupert Island, Canada	7:00 AM	5:00 PM
10-Aug	Sun	*At Sea*		
11-Aug	Mon	Victoria, Canada	8:00 AM	11:00 PM
12-Aug	Tue	Seattle, Washington	7:00 AM	

PROLOGUE

▼

Friday Afternoon
1st of August
3:11 PM PDT

Alec DunBarton entered Room 1401 at The Warwick Hotel in Seattle with two suitcases. He and Paige had just spent the last two months vacationing in California and now planned to take a nine-day Alaskan cruise with her immediate family.

With them are Paige's brother and sister-in-law, who own a successful catering business in Cupertino, California. The cruise was arranged by the Silicon Valley and San Francisco chapters of the American Catering Association to help its members become familiar with Pacific Northwest cuisine.

As Alec set down the bags, he murmured to Paige, "Let's go on the balcony. The desk clerk said we can see Puget Sound from there."

Paige followed her husband. As he slid open the glass door, she breathed in the crisp air and sighed, "It's nice out here. I wish I felt better. I think I'm getting a cold. I couldn't stop sneezing at the airport, and my throat is pretty sore."

Alec touched Paige's forehead. "I think you may have a fever. Did you pack any aspirin?"

Miserably, Paige shook her head. "We used them all. Would you mind if I lie down for a while?"

Alec helped Paige remove her shoes as she settled down on the left side of the bed and said, "I'm sure there's a pharmacy nearby. I'll pick up some Tylenol and Nyquil Cold & Flu medicine. Should I get you anything else?"

Paige thought a moment and responded, "Pick up some Cold-Eeze lozenges. They contain zinc and are supposed to shorten the duration of colds. I'm also thirsty. Can you get me a big bottle of water?"

Looking around the room, Alec noticed a small one on the hotel's mini fridge. Despite being listed for six dollars, Alec unscrewed the top and urged. "Start on this one."

After kissing Paige's brow, he added, "I'll see if your dad wants to stretch his legs."

Alec returned seconds later with Paige's father, Russell Anderson. He and Paige's Aunt Irena had a hotel room opposite theirs.

Concerned for his daughter, Russell felt her forehead and pronounced, "I'm also worried about Irena. She had a bad fall at the airport that left her with several bad bruises.

Paige muttered, "I can't believe she didn't break anything. She missed the first rung on the escalator and surfed down the steps on her suitcase!"

Russell grimaced. "She's icing her swollen knee right now. Water is leaking out of the plastic bag she's using. I want to pick her up a real ice bag."

In response, Paige suggested, "You two had better leave. I'm going to close my eyes for a few minutes and then check in on Irena. I hope that Derek and Jill are doing okay. Oliver didn't enjoy the flight over from San Jose. His poor ears were clogged, and Jill thinks his first tooth is coming in."

Alec acknowledged, "We'd better stop by their hotel room and see if they need something for Oliver."

As Alec softly closed the door behind them, he complained, "Some trip, so far!"

Alec and Russell found a Target near the Pike Place Market. Along the way, they passed by many homeless men and women. Alec shook his head in dismay and commented to his father-in-law, "It's a pity the city hasn't been able to address the problem effectively. Seattle is situated in a beautiful spot, and it could be a bustling metropolis again."

Russell agreed as they entered the discount store. After taking the escalator to the second floor, Alec had to look for a sales clerk to open the locked-up cold remedies. They were sitting behind pristine glass cases.

From another section, the clerk retrieved baby products for teething and earache pain. The only thing *not* under lock and key were old-fashioned ice bags. Before leaving, the two men picked up cubed cantaloupe and several bottles of water. They departed Target with a red and white reusable plastic bag full of health products.

Once back in The Warwick Hotel, the pair took the elevator to the fourteenth floor. Their first stop was Room 1407, where Derek and Gail Anderson were staying. Holding a smiling baby, Derek met them at the door and whispered, "Gail is taking a nap. She didn't get much sleep last night."

Derek took the medicine from Alec's hand and explained, "Oliver feels better now. I hope he doesn't get fussy again."

Though Alec knew his suggestion would be rebuffed, he professed, "My mother used to soothe my sore gums with Scotch. It never did me any harm."

Derek laughed, "Gail may not want to try it, but I'm all in favor of having a hefty glass of whisky before bedtime."

After a bit more discussion, it was decided that everyone should get together at 6:00 PM for dinner at Warwick's restaurant. The eatery's posted menu had plenty of meals at a moderate price."

The men separated in the corridor—Russell to check in on his sister and Alec to bring Paige her cold remedies. Upon sliding the plastic keycard into his door, Alec was surprised to see the room empty.

He was about to reenter the hall when Russell approached and stated, "They're chatting in my room. I'm going to get some fresh ice from the machine, and Paige has asked for you."

Alec hurried over to 1402 and was relieved to see his wife sitting up on the chaise lounge by the French balcony. Paige looked a little less pale and said, "I didn't know what was worse, worrying about Irena or possibly giving her my cold."

Irena, a year older than Russell, gushed, "Stuff and nonsense. I've had colds before, and if I can't spend time with my favorite niece, what's the point of living? We'll all probably have it by the end of the cruise."

Alec agreed but silently hoped that Paige's cold would run its course quickly. Although Irena appeared to be fragile, she was anything but. Her soft voice exuded strength and clarity. Her blue eyes took in everything around her. Beneath her demure façade, Aunt Irena was sharp-witted and self-reliant.

Irena gazed at her brother when he entered their room with a full ice bag. She gingerly placed it on her swollen knee and declared, "I've been icing it twenty minutes on and off. I should be good as new by tomorrow."

Russell, less sure, suggested, "Take it easy tonight and keep your leg elevated. I'll bring you dinner from the hotel's restaurant."

Paige, downing thirty milliliters of the cherry cold and flu medicine, asked, "Can you pick me up something, too? I should be hungry by dinnertime.

Alec agreed and noted, "It's 4:45 PM now. Do you know what you'll want to eat?"

He handed Paige the restaurant's handout containing the menu's QR code. After opening the link with her cell phone, Paige read, "There are soups, appetizers, salads, sandwiches, and main dishes."

Paige stopped to cough, and Irena answered, "I'd like a club sandwich if they have one and a dessert."

Alec was not surprised to hear Aunt Irena order a sweet. When he and Paige helped her run her bed and breakfast in Boothbay Harbor, Maine, she served her guests a wide variety of homemade baked goods.

The Warwick's desserts included triple-layer chocolate cake, caramel apple pie, and cherry cheesecake. Irena chose the last one. Paige had more difficulty picking something for herself and finally decided on tomato soup and a grilled cheese sandwich.

Upon making a choice, Alec had Paige return to their room. From previous experience, he knew Paige would grow sleepy from the nighttime Nyquil.

It took seconds for Alec to make his wife comfortable. While she dozed off, Alec put away the foodstuffs from Target and the clothing the couple planned to wear over the next two days.

With nothing to occupy his attention, Alec headed to the hotel's bar for a soft drink and to look over the American Catering Association's group activity list that Derek had given him earlier.

After being served, Alec removed the schedule from his pocket and read:

American Catering Association
Scheduled Activities

Date	Pegasus Itinerary	ACA Activites	Suggested ACA Excursions
Sunday 3rd of August	**Seattle, Washington:** Depart 3:00pm **Pugent Sound** Scenic Cruising	**Sail-Away Party for SV Caterers,** *Constellation Room: 5:00pm to 6:00pm* **SV Evening Meal,** *Britannia Dining Room: 6:00pm* **Sail-Away Party for SF Caterers,** *Constellation Room: 6:00pm to 7:00pm* **SF Evening Meal,** *Britannia Dining Room: 7:00pm*	
Monday 4th of August	**At Sea**	**Joint ACA Morning Meeting,** *Explorer's Club: 10:00am to 11:00am* **SV Dinner with the Executive Chef,** *Culinary Arts Center: 6:00pm to 10:00pm*	

The Singing Sleuth Gets Snowed Under

Date	Pegasus Itinerary	ACA Activites	Suggested ACA Excursions
Tuesday 5th of August	**Stephens Passage:** Scenic Cruising **Juneau, Alaska:** Arrive 1:00pm, Depart 9:00pm	**Joint ACA Morning Meeting,** *Explorer's Club: 10:00am to 11:00am* **See Excursions**	Alaskan Salmon Bake Bike & Brew Glacier View Evening Whale Quest Featuring Alaskan Cuisine Gold Panning Adventure and Salmon Bake Juneau Culinary Walk: In Partnership with Food & Wine Magazine Mendenhall Glacier, Fish Hatchery, & Salmon Bake Mendenhall Glacier, Kayak, & Salmon Bake Taku Lodge, Feast & Five Glacier Seaplane Disc.
Wednesday 6th of August	**Endicott Arm/Dawes Glacier:** Scenic Viewing	**SF ACA Afternoon Meeting,** *Hudson Room: 1:00pm to 1:45pm* **SV ACA Afternoon Meeting,** *Hudson Room: 2:00pm to 2:45pm* **SF Dinner with the Executive Chef,** *Culinary Arts Center: 6:00pm to 10:00pm*	
Thursday 7th of August	**Sitka, Alaska:** Arrive 8:00am, Depart 4:00pm	**See Excursions** **SV ACA Evening Meal,** *Rainbow Grill: 6:00pm to 8:00pm* **Food Trivia Game,** *Constellation Room: 9:00pm to 9:45pm*	Alaska Remote Fly Fishing & Shoreside Lunch Alaska Zodiac Adventure & Fin Island Lodge: In Partnership with Food & Wine Magazine Sitka Food Lover's Tour: In Partnership with Food & Wine Magazine Sitka Pedal & Pub Crawl
Friday 8th of August	**Ketchikan, Alaska:** Arrive 7:00am, Depart 6:00pm	**See Excursions**	Authentic Alaskan Bottom-Fishing Bering Sea Crab Hunt & Tasting Crab Expedition Wildlife Cruise & King Crab Snack Exclusive Coastal Cruise & Oyster Farm with Ocean-to-Table Tasting: Flightseeing & A Taste of Alaska Ketchikan Pub Crawl Off-Road UTV Safari, Cruise, Crab & Craft Beers The Great Alaskan Lumberjack Show & Crab Fest Cultural Showcase, Native Crafts & Culinary Tasting Wilderness Cruise & Silverking Lodge Seafood Fest Wilderness Exploration Cruise & Crab Fest
Saturday 9th of August	**Prince Rupert Island, Canada:** Arrive 7:00am, Depart 5:00pm	**See Excursions**	Chef Guided Gastronomy Tour Cow Bay Sights and Bites Taste of Prince Rupert Trolley Wheelhouse Brewery, Exclusive Access
Sunday 10th of August	**At Sea**	**Joint ACA Morning Meeting,** *Hudson Room: 11:30am to 12:30pm* **SF/SV Culinary Competition** *Culinary Arts Center: 2:00pm to 3:30pm* **Joint ACA Dinner,** *Bulldog Pub: 6:00pm to 7:30pm*	
Monday 11th of August	**Victoria, Canada:** *Arrive 8:00am, Depart 11:00pm*	**See Excursions** **Joint ACA Farewell Cocktail Party,** *Explorer's Club: 8:00pm to 9:00pm*	A Taste of Victoria Afternoon Tea at the Empress Hotel Chinatown and Old Town Tour and Tastings Craft Brewery Experience Grand City Drive & Empress Hotel High Tea Grand City Drive & Pendray Mansion High Tea Guided Pub Crawl with Ferry Ride & Appetizers Victoria Bites and Sights Victoria Culinary Walk: In Partnership with Food & Wine Magazine
Tuesday, 12th of August	**Seattle Washington:** Arrive 7:00am		

Alec was surprised to see how many of the ship's excursions offered food-related tours. There were pub crawls, culinary walks, and seafood feasts in nearly every port-of-call. Alec was reviewing the last few activities when he heard a raised voice come from the hotel's reception area.

From his seat, Alec caught sight of a large individual. He looked like a weight lifter and was dressed in a tight-fitting black t-shirt that showed off his bulging arm muscles. In a less-than-cultured British accent, the man complained, "I want to change rooms. There's a crying baby on the floor."

Under his breath, he muttered, "Babies have no business staying at a hotel. They should be at home where no one can hear their caterwauling."

Alec assumed he was ranting about Oliver and was the ACA member that Derek had warned him about.

His suspicions were confirmed when the flustered desk clerk replied, "Mr. Irwin, I understood your chapter of the American Catering Association wanted rooms on the same story. Would you prefer an executive suite on the twelfth floor?"

Sneering, he retorted, "I'll take it as long as it doesn't cost more."

As she handed him the new keycard, the woman gave her onlookers a helpless look.

Over the next forty-two hours, things went from bad to worse. On Saturday morning, Alec and Derek visited the Pike Place Market and developed a nasty stomach virus.

Alec blamed it on the crowds of people who had bumped into them as they walked past stalls of fresh fish, butchered meats, produce, flowers, and crafts. By Sunday morning, both men didn't know which end was up.

Despite the family's various illnesses, the group managed to check out of The Warwick Hotel by 11:00 AM. Paige's sore throat had turned into a full-fledged summer cold. Irena located new blueish-green bruises on her lower back and thigh. And Alec, weak from his stomach bug, had no desire to do anything but replenish lost liquids and sleep.

Russell, the only one feeling well, had to return to the drugstore several times to buy Imodium and drinks containing electrolytes. Gail found her hands full caring for a teething baby and a sick husband.

When the DunBartons and Andersons finally boarded the Pegasus at the Port of Seattle, they hurried off to their cabins on the Lower Promenade Deck to unpack and rest. Alec and Paige were happy to be back in their oversized cabin.

Their quarters contained a living room large enough to accommodate six people and a modest kitchenette that served as a dining area. A few pieces of well-placed furniture hid the couple's bedroom and bathroom from the rest of their lodgings.

Like many passenger cabins on the Lower Promenade Deck, the cabins had two doors—one leading to the inside corridor and the other to the promenade deck. The Pegasus advertised these accommodations as Prom Cabins.

Before emptying their suitcases, Paige headed over to the microwave in their kitchen to heat water for tea. Not ready to face the task either, Alec brought down two mugs from the upper cabinet and said, "I think I'd better have one, too."

Paige agreed. "It's important for you to stay hydrated." Wistfully, she added, "It's good to be back home and on vacation till August 12th. It will give us time to get better and readjust."

While sipping their hot teas, Alec admitted, "I hope no one gets murdered on this cruise. Right now, food isn't even appealing!"

Alec's statement left Paige momentarily flabbergasted.

CHAPTER ONE

▼

"Celebration"

Words & Music by Eumir Deodato, Ronald Bell,
Earl Toon, George Brown, James Taylor, Dennis Thomas,
Robert Bell, Robert Mickens, and Claydes Smith
Genre: Post Disco, Released: October 1980

Sunday Afternoon—3rd of August

At half past four, Alec's curiosity got the better of him, and he asked Paige, "Would you mind if I go to the Constellation Room at five? The Silicon Valley caterers are holding their Sail-Away Party there."

Taking a sip of her second cup of herbal tea, Paige insisted, "Don't worry about me. I ordered chicken soup from room service. It should get here soon. Later, my dad and aunt plan to come by. Right now, they're watching Oliver so that Derek and Gail can attend the party and group dinner."

Assured that Paige would be fine, Alec relented, "I won't be gone long. I'd like to match the names of the American Catering Associates with the descriptions Derek gave me."

In response to Paige's question about his dinner plans, Alec admitted, "My stomach is still unsettled. I plan to order ginger ale at the bar and get a bowl of plain pasta from the Lido buffet. I hope my appetite returns tomorrow."

Paige giggled and then coughed, "I'm sure it will."

Alec kissed Paige's brow, glad she was no longer feverish, and headed out the door.

The Constellation Room was one of Alec's favorite haunts. It was located on the Observation Deck and surrounded by floor-to-ceiling bay windows. During the day, passengers were treated to incredible ocean views, and at night, small bright lights in the domed ceiling sparkled in the configuration of constellations.

Upon arriving at the hotspot, Alec was waved over by Douglas Abbot, the ship's doctor. Alec was thrilled to see his closest friend on the Pegasus. After catching up on the last two months, Alec mentioned that Paige had a summer cold, and he was getting over a twenty-four-hour bug.

Candidly, Alec revealed, "I plan to keep a watchful eye on the American Catering Association this evening. I don't know if my stomach virus is making me queasy or I just have a bad feeling about … the group."

Alec was finishing his sentence when two women entered the lounge with the bodybuilder. One was beautiful and in her fifties. She had on a tight black gown that showed off her shapely breasts. Though the other woman was about ten years older, fifty pounds heavier, and in a frumpy dress, she appeared to be comfortable in her own skin.

Alec whispered to Douglas, "The femme fatale in the group is Bella Valentino. She was born in Italy and is the president of the Silicon Valley chapter. She arranged this cruise with the San Francisco ACA members."

When the threesome entered a private room adjoining the lounge, Douglas asked, "Who's that big guy?"

Alec grumbled, "He's Derek's main competitor. His name is Robert Irwin. He caters to people who want to decrease body fat and become more muscular."

The doctor shook his head. "I think he's a walking time bomb. I've met men like him before, and I'm quite certain he's on anabolic steroids."

"That can't be good," Alec remarked. "The other woman is Nancy Lawton. She makes low-calorie desserts for Derek's company, 'Deliteful Dinners and Desserts.' When Paige and I were staying with the Andersons, I sampled several of her baked goods and must say, they were delicious."

Eager to see who else was a member of the Silicon Valley club, Alec suggested to Douglas, "Let's crash their party."

Even though the doctor was reluctant, the two men joined the group and were greeted by Derek and Gail. In a loud voice, Derek introduced the newcomers to his fellow caterers and announced, "Meet my brother-in-law, Alec DunBarton. He's the controller on the ship. With him is Douglas Abbot, the ship's physician. I had the pleasure of meeting the doctor a few years ago at my sister's wedding in Inverness, Scotland."

Alec had forgotten that Derek and Douglas had met before and was glad the partygoers seemed okay with their presence. Robert Irwin shook Alec's hand almost too heartily.

The room became lively when the DJ played "Celebration" by Kool and the Gang. Before he could stop himself, Alec sang along with the 1980s hit,

Yahoo!
Celebration
Yahoo!
This is your celebration

Celebrate good times, come on!
(Let's celebrate)
Celebrate good times, come on!
(Let's celebrate)

There's a party goin' on right here
A celebration to last throughout the years
So bring your good times and your laughter too
We gonna celebrate your party with you

Come on now, celebration
Let's all celebrate and have a good time

Celebration
We gonna celebrate and have a good time

It's time to come together
It's up to you, what's your pleasure?
Everyone around the world come on!

Yahoo!
It's a celebration
Yahoo!

Celebrate good times, come on!
(It's a celebration)
Celebrate good times, come on!
(Let's celebrate)

There's a party goin' on right here
A dedication to last throughout the years
So bring your good times and your laughter too
We gonna celebrate and party with you

Come on now, celebration
Let's all celebrate and have a good time, yeah yeah
Celebration
We gonna celebrate and have a good time

It's time to come together
It's up to you, what's your pleasure?
Everyone around the world come on!

Afterward, Alec was introduced to several Silicon Valley ACA members. It included Jeffrey Webber, his daughter Brett, Mei Chung, and Carlos Ruiz.

Alec was able to size them up in seconds. Jeffrey appeared tightly wound, wearing a suit jacket and a bowtie. According to Derek, the fellow had taught at a prestigious cooking school and moved to the West Coast after his wife died to run a corporate catering business. His daughter, unlike her father, was extremely cordial. Her plump cheeks were red and perspired as she made the rounds.

The other two individuals were from different culinary backgrounds. Mei Chung was raised in China, taught in France, and worked as a private chef for a family in Palo Alto. She was with an animated young man named Carlos Ruiz.

Gail pulled Alec aside to introduce him to Bella Valentino. Up close, she was even more of a temptress. When she walked away, Alec asked his sister-in-law about Carlos and was told, "He's responsible for making Irwin's company a success and has been unable to break his contract with him. The two have been ignoring each other since we boarded. Irwin is a nasty character, and Ruiz has a short fuse."

Deciding to keep an eye on them, Alec sipped his ginger ale. The remainder of the cocktail hour went smoothly. When the Silicon Valley party ended, Derek invited Alec and Douglas to join the group in the Britannia Dining Room for dinner.

The pair turned Derek down. Douglas had a standing dinner date with Alec's assistant, Regina Hill. And Alec didn't want to be away from Paige too long.

With a tray containing a dish of plain spaghetti, four crunchy rolls, and a dessert of bread pudding, Alec approached his suite. Paige must have heard him fumbling at the door and greeted him as he crossed the threshold.

Paige took the tray from him with a smile and said, "I'm feeling better now."

About to scold her for getting out of bed, Alec relented and asked, "Have you had enough to eat? I've brought down some extra rolls and butter.

Taking one from the plate, she replied, "This is perfect. I'm going to run my bath. After you have dinner, tell me about your evening."

While Paige filled the tub with effervescent bath gel, Alec ate his bland meal. He didn't want to have anything too rich and experience a second episode of gastric distress.

After finishing his bread puffing, Alec joined Paige in the bathroom and watched her luxuriate in the tub of foamy bubbles.

Over the next twenty minutes, he repeated the conversations he and Douglas had with the caterers.

Alec had just completed his report when he heard a knock and hurried to the door. Paige's aunt, dad, and nephew greeted him. Oliver looked very cute in his giraffe-print pajamas. Russell put him down on the floor so he could crawl and asked, "How is everyone feeling?"

Paige emerged from the bathroom wrapped in a robe and answered, "I'm much less tired. The ship is at sea tomorrow, and I plan to baby my cold. What are you guys going to do?"

Irena replied, "I looked at the ship's activities. Your dad and I hope to attend the Alaska Up Close lecture: Pacific Giants, at ten. It should be very informative. Later, there will be presentations on wildlife viewing and shore excursions."

Aware that they may not get a chance to do everything they hoped, Paige offered, "Let us know if you can't babysit. Alec and I can watch Oliver, too."

Laughing, Alec bent down to give Oliver a bunch of stackable plastic measuring cups from the kitchen. As he occupied himself with his new toy, Alec confirmed, "I can't wait to show him off to the ship's staff."

Upon checking his watch, Russell picked up his grandson and said, "We promised to put Oliver to bed by seven. We don't want to be accused of spoiling the lad."

When their guests departed, the DunBartons got ready for bed. Eager to wash off any remaining gastroenteritis germs, Alec showered while Paige watched an old Hitchcock film among the ship's streamed movies. Alec slipped into bed as she began to doze off. Within minutes, Alec was also dead to the world.

Alec and Paige awakened to the sound of someone rapping on their door. Paige looked at their bedside clock and squealed, "It's nearly ten o'clock. I can't believe we slept so long!"

Wrapping her discarded robe around her, she let in Derek, Gail, and Oliver. Profusely, Gail apologized for waking the couple, and

Derek explained, "Dad and Aunt Irena went to a lecture about Humpback and Orca whales.

"Could you watch Oliver during our ACA morning meeting? One of the excursion team members is going to tell us about their tours and what we can expect to learn about Pacific Northwest cuisine on this cruise."

Immediately, Paige put his concerns aside and promised, "We'll take good care of him."

Not waiting for his sister to change her mind, Derek pushed Oliver's stroller into the room. Gail pointed out the diaper bag on the handle and explained, "It contains diapers, wipes, ointments, empty baby bottles, and extra clothes."

As they turned to leave, Derek said, "We should be back in an hour or two."

For the remainder of the morning, Alec and Paige entertained Oliver. While Paige showered, Alec sat the young fellow on the bed and put on the Food Network. It was one of the few channels the ship carried live. While the chefs displayed their cooking prowess, Oliver played with nestled plastic measuring spoons and cups.

When Paige emerged from the bathroom, ready for the day, she sniffed the air and cautioned, "I think we need to change someone's diaper."

Alec laughed and pointed to Oliver. The diaper change turned out to be a big ordeal. The pair were forced to bathe, diaper, and redress the lad in clean clothes. By the time Oliver's parents returned, Alec and Paige were ready for a nap.

Glad to have a spotless child back, Derek invited the twosome to dinner, declaring, "Tonight, my group is dining with the ship's executive chef and will be treated to a seven-course meal paired with wine. Two people from our chapter weren't able to sail with us, and we thought of you. The meal is going to be served in the Culinary Arts Center from 6:00 PM to 10:00 PM and is only open to a few participants."

Alec, who missed breakfast and had regained his appetite, was thrilled. Now eager to return to the land of the living, Alec convinced Paige to join him for a small lunch on the Lido Deck. He planned to save room for what he expected to be the highlight of the cruise.

CHAPTER TWO

▼

"Food, Glorious Food"
Words & Music by Lionel Bart
Genre: Broadway Musical (*Oliver*), Released: January 1968

Monday Evening—4th of August

Alec and Paige took great care in getting ready for the evening. The Pegasus was having its first dress-up night. Since the DunBartons weren't expected to attend the Captain's Welcome Gala for another week, they used their free time to prepare for the executive chef's seven-course dinner.

After checking that Alec was well-attired, Paige slipped on her black heels, which accentuated her shapely long legs. Although Alec was eager to leave, he couldn't help admiring his wife in her red and black strapless gown.

On the way to the Culinary Arts Center, Alec revealed, "I've met Executive Chef Claude Bourdain a few times but have said little to him. He transferred here a few months back and has a terrific reputation. I understand he's a master at combining food and wine."

Paige nodded, less interested in food than her husband. She mostly enjoyed baked goods such as rolls, pastries, muffins, and croissants. Her favorite meal was breakfast, where she could indulge in them to her heart's content.

A few minutes to six, Alec and Paige entered the Culinary Arts Center. They were the first to arrive. Paige pointed out the long oval table set for twelve people and declared, "I'm glad we won't make an unlucky thirteen." Smaller tables held glasses and bottles of room-temperature and chilled wines.

Waitstaff and assistant chefs were on hand to answer questions and distribute the evening's menu. Alec took one and read:

Menu for Executive Chef's Meal

Amuse Bouche
"Domaine St. Michelle Brut, Washington State"

Warm scallop, walnut, and calves liver salad
Lightly sautéed in garlic with fresh herbs,
finished with raspberry vinegar reduction
served over a crisp spinach and vegetable salad
"Leonard Kreusch Riesling Spatlese Piesporter
Michelsberg"

Seafood Terrine
Lobster medallions and crab leg set in a light salmon mousse,
garnished with caviar and served with basil tomato sauce
"D.O. Rioja, Marques de Caceres"

Mock Turtle Soup
Double beef consommé flavored with turtle herbs
and topped with a curry liaison
"Ruffino Pinot Grigio, Italy"

Lattice of Halibut and Salmon
Served on watercress with herb sauce
"Franciscan Chardonnay Valley, California"

Orange Sorbet with Champagne

Sautéed Fillet of Sterling Beef Tenderloin
Filled with Stilton cheese, served
with a rich Madeira and tarragon reduction,
garlic mashed potato, grilled tomato, and broccoli puree
"Spellbound Petit-Sirah, California"

Claude's Crème Brulé
A decadent classic dessert like the old days
"Dow's Late Bottle Vintage Port, Portugal"

Alec looked up from the list of seven-course dishes when Gail and Derek filed in, followed by their fellow caterers. With Derek's help, Alec recalled their names. The group included Bella, Robert, Nancy, Jeffrey, Brett, Mei, and Carlos.

Bob Irwin was the person who interested Alec the most. The man was dressed informally in the same black t-shirt he had previously worn. He showed more disdain for the proceedings when the executive chef entered the room and refused to clap with the others.

Over the next four hours, Alec ate a great deal, drank even more, and noted that the Silicon Valley caterers had issues relating to one another. Hands down, the person with the biggest ego was the weight lifter.

Irwin knew Claude Bourdain from when they both sailed on the Aquarius, a ship in the Flagship Cruise Line fleet. After having a heated conversation, the two men said little to each other for the remainder of the evening. Irwin refused to have a drop of wine and made snide remarks about several dishes.

Bella Valentino, wearing a dress with a plunging neckline, paid attention to every word Claude uttered and eyed Bob when he said mean-spirited things about the food. By the end of the dinner, she had difficulty containing her anger towards him.

Instead of apologizing, Irwin growled, "I'm going to the gym to burn off this pretentious crap."

Alec soon learned that the executive chef had heard Bob's insulting remark and laughed it off, commenting, "Irwin has said much worse to me over the years. We look at food differently. I try to make dining a memorable experience, and he uses food to create powerful bodies."

While interacting with the diners, Alec discovered that Carlos Ruiz was taught to cook at his parent's bed and breakfast in Tucson, Arizona. The caterer had recently received a job offer for a sous chef position at a well-known restaurant in San Francisco. Carlos was forced to turn it down when Irwin threatened him with a breach of contract.

Brett had other issues with Robert Irwin. When she began to serve international comfort foods from her food truck, the bodybuilder reported her to the Fire Department. His actions delayed her startup and caused her father, Jeffrey Webber, to break most remaining ties with him.

Alec didn't get much of an opportunity to speak to Mei Chung. Every time he tried to engage her in conversation, she had a wine glass inches from her mouth. She was pretty intoxicated by the end of the function.

The easiest person to get to know was Nancy Lawton. She was born and raised on a dairy farm in New York State. Since Paige's grandparents had also been brought up on a farm, they had plenty to talk about.

By dessert, Alec could not take another bite. When the DunBartons set off for their cabin, the tune from the Broadway production of *Oliver* came to Alec's mind. In his tenor voice, he sang out.

Food, glorious food!
Hot sausage and mustard!
While we're in the mood
Cold jelly and custard!
Pease pudding and saveloys!
What next is the question?
Rich gentlemen have it, boys
In-di-gestion!

Food, glorious food!
We're anxious to try it.
Three banquets a day
Our favourite diet!

Just picture a great big steak
Fried, roasted or stewed.
Oh, food,
Wonderful food,
Marvelous food,
Glorious food.

Food, glorious food!
Eat right through the menu.
Just loosen your belt
Two inches and then you
Work up a new appetite.
In this interlude
The food,
Once again, food
Fabulous food,
Glorious food.

Food, glorious food!
Don't care what it looks like—
Burned!
Underdone!

Crude!
Don't care what the cook's like.
Just thinking of growing fat
Our senses go reeling
One moment of knowing that
Full-up feeling!

Food, glorious food!
What wouldn't we give for
That extra bit more—
That's all that we live for
Why should we be fated to
Do nothing but brood
On food,
Magical food,
Wonderful food,
Marvelous food,
Fabulous food

Upon entering their suite, Alec tossed off his dress shoes and slid onto their bed, groaning, "I never want to eat again!"

In response, Paige giggled.

CHAPTER THREE

"Cold as Ice"
Words & Music by Lou Gramm and Mic Jones
Genre: Synth Rock, Released: July 1977

Tuesday Morning—5th of August

Alec and Paige were suddenly awakened at 5:20 AM. Paige heard the knocking first and was halfway to the door when Alec grumbled, "Who can that be at this hour!"

Paige stood back as the Chief of Security, Harold Zuma, entered the room. The South African officer was tall, black, and in his mid-fifties. Zuma had transferred to the Pegasus a year and a half earlier.

The officer's expression was bleak as he uttered, "A passenger was just found dead in the fitness center. We cordoned off the area, and Dr. Abbot is tending to him now. Please come right away."

It took Alec seconds to throw on some clothes and grab his cell phone. Though it wasn't unusual for elderly passengers to die on the Pegasus, Alec couldn't ignore the bad feeling welling up in his gut.

Eager to see whether it was the person he suspected, Alec hurried to the elevator and up to the Lido Deck with Zuma. A few passengers were standing behind the security team's blockade.

When a guard saw Alec and Harold approach, he moved aside to give them access.

The gym took up the ship's bow and had floor-to-ceiling windows facing the ocean. Assorted pieces of exercise equipment stood along the circumference of the glass-enclosed room like soldiers ready to battle.

Alec wasn't much of an exerciser. He had only been to the fitness center on a handful of occasions. The first was when Mark Linley, the former controller on the Pegasus, was murdered. His untimely death gave Alec a reason to leave England, escape past heartache, and recreate his life at sea.

The deceased person was on the bench press. Dr. Abbot was hovering over the individual when Alec's eyes descended on him. When he drew closer, Alec's worst fears were realized. The body belonged to Robert Irwin, the ACA caterer and weight lifter.

Turning to Alec, Douglas relayed, "It looks like the fellow's hand slipped while lifting an inordinate amount of weight."

Alec looked down at Irwin. The steal bar of the dumbbell was pressed against his throat. It wasn't a pretty sight, and Alec assumed he had died quickly.

Although Douglas wanted to get him to sickbay immediately, Alec made him wait while he took photos of the bench press, the deceased, and his belongings. Two of Zuma's men had to lift the barbell off the body and onto the j hook. Once the corpse was unencumbered, Alec took more pictures.

Minutes later, Douglas had the security men place Irwin on a rollable stretcher and set off for the crew elevator. While departing with Zuma, the doctor called, "I'll be in the ship's morgue. I want to examine the corpse thoroughly and determine when Irwin might have passed away."

Alec nodded, concerned that Irwin's death was *not* accidental. He had a million questions. Did the ship's security cameras capture the accident? What were the fitness center's hours? And did Irwin go to the gym directly after the four-hour dinner at the Culinary Arts Center?

Just as Alec gathered Irwin's towel and trousers, the men's fitness instructor entered the gym. From his expression, Alec could see he was troubled. Unbelievingly, he protested, "I can't believe Mr. Irwin had an accident. I met him on the first night of the cruise. He signed our waiver and knew how to use all the equipment.

"Mr. Irwin came at closing time last night and said he needed to work out a few hours. He was adamant about staying, and I told him to lock up when he finished his routine." Counting the weight on the bench press bar, the fellow added, "It's at 315 pounds. I've seen him lift more than that."

Unsure how dangerous it was for Irwin to use the equipment without a spotter, Alec asked, and the fitness instructor confessed, "I should have stayed with him."

Alec let him resume his regular duties as the gym was scheduled to open at six. Early risers were already waiting to get in. Before leaving with Irwin's possessions, Alec warned the instructor, "Someone with security will take your statement today."

From the fitness center, Alec hurried down to the ship's morgue. As he approached the room, he could hear voices. Because Flagship Cruise Line catered to elderly clientele, who sometimes came aboard with heart disease and other life-threatening ailments, the Pegasus had cold storage for six persons.

The morgue also contained a stainless-steel table and various instruments and medical devices. The doctor was taking the corpse's temperature when Alec joined him and Officer Zuma.

On seeing Alec, Douglas stated, "I think he died between 11:00 PM and 1:00 AM. Each hour, the body temperature falls about 1.5 degrees Fahrenheit until it reaches room temperature. When circulation ceases, blood starts to pool and settle. Rigor mortis sets in about two to six hours after death."

When Zuma muttered, "This one is as cold as ice," Alec sang,

You're as cold as ice
You're willing to sacrifice our love

You never take advice
Someday you'll pay the price, I know

I've seen it before
It happens all the time
You're closing the door
You leave the world behind

You're digging for gold
Yet throwing away
A fortune in feelings
But someday you'll pay

You're as cold as ice
You're willing to sacrifice our love
You want Paradise
But someday you'll pay the price
I know

I've seen it before
It happens all the time
You're closing the door
You leave the world behind
You're digging for gold
Yet throwing away
A fortune in feelings
But someday you'll pay

Cold as ice, you know that you are
Cold, (cold) as, (as) ice,
As cold as ice to me
(Cold, cold cold) (as, as, as) (ice)

Captain Stewart entered the morgue just as Alec finished the last verse. Hoping he hadn't been overheard, Alec stammered, "This one may be an accident."

Douglas, examining the corpse's extremities with a high-powered magnifier, interrupted, "Not so fast. There's old scar tissue on his deltoids, vastus lateralis, and gluteus, probably from injected anabolic steroids."

Concentrating on a spot near the decedent's hairline, the doctor added, "This injection mark is recent. Initially, it looked like Irwin died when the barbell compressed his neck and cut off his oxygen supply. Now, I'm not certain his death was accidental."

The captain gazed at Alec with a look that could kill and ordered, "View the gym's surveillance footage, contact authorities in Juneau, Alaska, and take care of it! Let me know what they say and how they plan to handle this mess."

Quickly, Stewart exited the morgue. He had only been on the ship for nine months. Despite being bald and of average weight and height, he commanded respect. His blue eyes had a way of delving into your very soul.

Glad they were alone again, Alec donned a pair of medical gloves and unwrapped the items he found beside Irwin's body. Alec had gathered them up in a second towel to prevent contamination. The bodybuilder's towel did not feel wet, and when Alec sniffed it, he decided it hadn't been used.

Carefully, Alec reached into Irwin's trouser pockets and brought out his keycard. The pants were the ones he had worn the previous evening, and Alec surmised that the weight lifter came to dinner with exercise shorts under his trousers. There were no sharp objects in the gym that could have made the injection mark on his neck.

Alec and Zuma hurried to the ship's surveillance room with more questions than answers. Cameras were situated all over the vessel to monitor the safety of its passengers and crew members. The footage was used to investigate accidents, train staff, and corroborate illegal activities.

When the officer on duty pulled up the video from the fitness center's three cameras, it was discovered that only two were operational. The working ones had caught Irwin near the towel rack, by the water fountain, and on several pieces of exercise equipment. Those cameras also captured the fitness instructor's movements up to 10:45 PM.

The remaining camera, which monitored the gym's entrance and bench presses, did not record anything. Furiously, Harold

Zuma shouted at the officer and instructed, "Look at past footage and tell me how long it's been out of commission."

After checking the system, the fellow reported, "Yesterday, it recorded a full day's activity. Something must have been placed over the camera lens. What do you want me to do?"

Zuma grunted, "I'll take care of it."

Minutes later, Alec and the security chief returned to the gym and learned that masking tape was covering the eye of the non-working camera. Concerned that the adhesive may contain fingerprints, Alec instructed Zuma to leave it alone and stated, "We'll be docking in Juneau at one o'clock. Please get in touch with the town's police department. The authorities will want to see it."

When the two separated in the corridor, Alec recalled the lyrics to "Cold as Ice" and wondered whether Robert Irwin had just paid the price for a past misdeed.

Alec's first stop was his cabin. Paige was having coffee with Irena when he arrived and asked, "Is Robert Irwin really dead? Was it an accident?"

Not surprised they heard about it, Alec replied, "Douglas found a pinprick of blood on Irwin's neck. It looks like he was injected with something, and his killer took steps to hide his or her presence in the fitness center. We're pretty sure he was murdered."

Alec, helping himself to coffee, resumed, "The man was a bully and nasty individual. I don't think we'll be short of suspects."

Excitedly, Aunt Irena declared, "We must help you investigate. Where do you want us to start?"

Pausing a moment, Alec suggested, "Would you mind going on the excursion that Nancy Lawton plans to take in Juneau? I'd like to know more about her."

Irena accepted the mission and asked, "Is she the one who makes those low-calorie and healthy desserts for Derek's company? I tried several of them at their house, and they were simply marvelous."

After confirming she was, Paige offered, "Who do you want me to befriend?"

Alec replied, "Bella Valentino. I can't get a handle on her, either. She's smart yet plays the vamp when men are around. I'll find out which excursions the ladies plan to take this afternoon and book you on them."

Noting the time, Alec finished his black coffee and headed for the door, explaining, "The ACA members are currently meeting in the Explorer's Club. I'd better have a word with them before they hear about Irwin's death through our grapevine."

The Explorer's Club was large enough to host the Silicon Valley and San Francisco ACA chapters. The lounge, decorated with nautical instruments and maritime artifacts from Flagship Cruise Line's earliest vessels, gave off a comfortable vibe.

When Alec entered the room, he immediately noticed platters of fruit, pastries, rolls, and cold cuts on the bar's counter. A bartender was busy preparing Mimosa and Bloody Mary cocktails for those who liked to have a mid-morning pick-me-up with their snacks.

The caterers were divided into two groups. While eating a crusty roll laden with a few slices of ham and cheese, Alec listened to the man in charge of the SF caterers. He was counting the members who planned to attend their upcoming dinner with the executive chef on Wednesday evening.

Bella's group was discussing the excursions offered in Juneau. While tallying their numbers, Alec finished his mini breakfast and dusted the crumbs off his shirt. It took some time for him to get the attention of both chapters.

When the background noise was less audible, Alec announced, "My name is Alec DunBarton. You may or may not know that I'm the controller on the Pegasus and ship's liaison officer, responsible for communication between Flagship Cruise Line and local police authorities.

"Having said that, I have the sad duty to tell you that Robert Irwin, a member of the ACA's Silicon Valley chapter, was found dead this morning in the gym. Over the next few days, I plan to speak to people who had direct contact with Mr. Irwin."

The San Francisco chapter members did not seem fazed by Alec's declaration. The president of their group replied, "We'll help you any way we can, but most of us have had limited contact, if any, with him."

Bella Valentino's members reacted more animatedly. Jeffrey Webber asked how he died, his daughter smiled like Mona Lisa, and Mei looked down at her hands. Nancy gasped loudly, and Carlos Ruiz muttered under his breath. "It couldn't have happened to a nicer guy."

Derek and Gail Anderson admitted to hearing about the bodybuilder's demise at the Lido buffet but were not totally surprised by the news. Deciding to concentrate on the people most familiar with Irwin's vices, Alec told the San Fransico caterers to go on with their scheduled meeting.

Addressing himself to Bella's group, Alec explained, "Mr. Irwin's hand may have slipped while using the bench press. It's also possible he had a coronary while exercising. The barbell shaft crushed his windpipe, and his death was probably instantaneous." Alec did *not* mention that he was murdered.

Before leaving, Alec asked the group what excursions they planned to take in Juneau and learned that Bella and Nancy were booked on the Mendenhall Glacier, Fish Hatchery, & Salmon Bake Tour.

Alec was happy to hear that Derek and Gail were going on the Juneau Culinary Walk with Brett, Mei, and Carlos and would be able to update him later. Only Jeffrey chose the exclusive Taku Lodge, Feast, & Five Glacier Seaplane Discovery Adventure.

Wondering how much the excursion was costing Jeffrey, Alec returned to his cabin. While Paige and Irena were chatting, he reserved two seats on the glacier trip and reminded them to keep track of their quarry, take plenty of pictures, and be on the pier by two thirty to meet their group.

Aware that his afternoon was going to be equally busy, Alec set off for the infirmary. He had a number of questions for the doctor.

CHAPTER FOUR

▼

"Alaska and Me"
Words & Music by John Denver
Genre: Folk Song, Released: June 1988

Tuesday Afternoon—5th of August

As hoped, Alec located Dr. Abbot in the infirmary. After waiting for him to finish up with a passenger with a middle ear infection, Alec asked the doctor how anabolic steroids affected people who used them.

Douglas invited Alec into his office since he was no longer on call for the morning. The room had floor-to-ceiling bookshelves filled with medical texts and dog-eared journals. Faded diplomas were on the opposite wall. While taking a seat behind his polished oak desk, Douglas asked, "So, what do you want to know?"

Selecting a leather chair near him, Alec posed. "Do you think someone injected an anabolic steroid into Irwin's neck?"

Douglas shook his head. "It's impossible to know from my cursory examination. Irwin had scar tissue in places where a bodybuilder would normally inject testosterone or other PEDs."

Alec stopped him and learned that PEDs stood for performing enhancing drugs, and they came in several forms—injections, pills, gels and creams, and implanted pellets. Douglas explained,

"I didn't see recent scar tissue. The decedent may have stopped using steroids or switched to another form, such as pills. From his muscle development, I would guess he was still on something when he died."

Douglas continued, "Enthusiasts can purchase illegal steroids from the internet and smugglers, who have brought them into the US from aboard. Some weight lifters, keen to build muscles quickly, take ten to hundred times the therapeutic dosages and use several different steroids at the same time."

"That can't be safe!" Alec exclaimed.

Douglas agreed, "It's not. Anabolic steroids have been known to cause medical, emotional, and psychological problems. Side effects include high blood pressure, blood clots, stroke, liver damage, and heart issues. Abusers can also experience 'roid rage,' in which they display violent tendencies such as anger, aggression, and, in worst cases, psychosis. Men may produce less sperm, see a decrease in their testicle size, and grow breasts."

Noting all the ill effects, Alec marveled aloud, "Why would anyone take them?"

Also confounded, the doctor replied, "Users may have body dysmorphia from childhood or young adulthood."

With more than enough information on anabolic steroids, Alec rose and thanked the good doctor. As he was about to leave, Alec's cell phone rang. Zuma was at the other end.

Turning to Douglas, Alec announced, "Harold has spoken to the Juneau Police Department. They're sending over two police officers at 1:30 PM. He wants us to meet them at the gangway. Will you be able to join me?"

Douglas answered in the affirmative and suggested. "We'd better get some lunch. There's no telling how long they'll need us."

Alec agreed despite telling Paige the previous evening that he never wanted to eat again. Together, the men took the elevator to the Lido Deck to have deli sandwiches, chips, and iced tea.

At 1:25 PM, Alec waited with Zuma and Dr. Abbot at the security kiosk beside the passenger gangway. Upon spying a fellow in a police uniform and a plainclothes woman, Alec pointed out, "That may be them. If it is, they're certainly punctual."

In moments, Alec's suspicions were confirmed. The woman approached the threesome and declared, "I'm the deputy chief at the Juneau Police Department. My name is Nicola Campbell."

Alec detected an accent and asked, "Did you grow up in Scotland? Glasgow?"

Giving Alec a warm smile, she replied, "My, you're good. And you? Were you raised in the Highlands? Inverness?"

Although Alec would have liked to talk about their homeland, he presented Chief of Security Zuma and Dr. Douglas Abbot. He added, "I'm Alec DunBarton, the controller on the Pegasus. On several occasions, I've been asked to act as liaison between the ship and outside law enforcement."

"Well," she chuckled, "you're in the right place at the right time. I brought Sergeant McGrath with me. We've had experience with shipboard crew that have misbehaved on our island, but this is a new one for us. Can you please take us to see the deceased?"

The doctor led the visitors to the morgue. Nicola, as she liked to be called, was eager to see the corpse. Douglas let her know that Irwin died sometime between 11:00 PM and 1:00 AM. He also showed her the pinprick injection mark at Irwin's hairline. The doctor remained behind to prepare the body for pick-up in a few hours.

The deputy chief had a strange way of saying things, and her facial expressions were endearing. She often held her head in a cocked position and narrowed her green eyes to catlike slits when she asked questions.

From the morgue, the Juneau officials followed Alec and Zuma to the fitness center. The gym was empty, and Alec suspected that many passengers were sightseeing. Since the body had been moved, Alec showed Nicola the crime scene photos he had taken and the masking tape, adhering to the surveillance camera.

In response, McGrath put on gloves and used a chair to remove the piece of tape. After placing it in an evidence bag, he asked, "Did the other two cameras capture anything?"

Zuma replied miserably, "Not much. I can show you the video footage after you speak to the fitness instructor."

Alec summoned the young man and had him repeat what he said earlier. On hearing that he left Irwin alone in the gym to finish his exercise routine, Nicola announced, "It's evident that Robert Irwin was murdered. Otherwise, there would have been no point in disabling the camera.

McGrath asked Zuma to show them to the security screening room next. After viewing the footage, Nicola questioned how Irwin's assailant could have placed masking tape on the camera without being seen.

The trio considered several possibilities and decided that the perpetrator must have found a blind spot and used a pole or cane to reach the surveillance equipment. Nicola also requested Alec to email her the digital photographs and all the fitness center video footage taken after the ship departed from Seattle. It was clear to Alec that she wanted to see if any passengers had shown undue interest in the cameras before Irwin's death.

Zuma escorted the group to Robert Irwin's quarters next and used his keycard to unlock the door. McGrath handed out gloves and asked Alec and Zuma to refrain from touching anything. Although Alec had conducted several searches independently, he was happy to let the deputy chief and sergeant take charge.

Over the next thirty minutes, they found Anavar pills in the bathroom and a stack of papers about the American Catering Association. Nicola placed them in an evidence bag and asked Alec about the ACA.

Alec explained, "Two local chapters of the catering organization are on this cruise to learn about Alaskan ingredients. The members are from San Francisco and Silicon Valley, California. My brother-in-law and his wife belong to the SV group and had a lot to say about Irwin. To be candid, the man was arrogant and had crossed several of his fellow caterers.

Nicola nodded, "I'd like to hear all about them. Right now, I need to have the decedent's corpse picked up and sent to our state's medical examiner in Anchorage. The office investigates deaths and performs autopsies when the deceased appears to be in good health, is not under a physician's care, and whose death resulted from accident, suicide, or homicide. Your corpse meets all those requirements."

The deputy chief instructed Harold Zuma to lock the cabin and have his men pack up Irwin's personal belongings. After exchanging phone numbers and email addresses, Zuma accompanied Detective McGrath to the passenger gangway. The officer had been tasked with arranging an exact pick-up time.

Upon hearing that Nicola Campbell planned to stay on the ship and get acquainted with the surroundings, Alec volunteered to show her around. Their last stop on the tour was the Lido buffet, where they each collected coffee and dessert.

Alec directed her to an outside table near the pool. Nicola smiled as she tasted the sweets, commenting about the flavors and possible ingredients. Alec could tell by her interest that she was a fellow foodie.

While sipping their drinks, Alec asked, "Is it usually this warm?"

The sun was streaming through the open glass enclosure as Nicola stretched like a kitten and responded, "It's not. Last week was awful, with rain and temperatures in the 50s. I understand it's going to be mild the entire week. Alaska can be so beautiful when the weather cooperates."

The two talked about their lives. Alec learned that she was a single mother and dating a child psychologist. She had moved from Glasgow twenty years earlier, fed up with the dirt and decay she had grown up in.

With a curious expression, she voiced, "There's a song by Bob Denver called 'Alaska and Me.' It perfectly expresses my feelings about my new homeland."

Wanting to hear the lyrics, Alec pressed her, and she sang softly,

When I was a child and I lived in the city
I dreamed of Alaska so far away
And I dreamed I was flying over mountains and glaciers
Somehow I knew that I'd live there one day.
Well it took me some growing, and a fair bit of schooling
And a little bit of trouble to get on the move
And I felt like a loser but I turned out the winner
When I came to Alaska the land that I love.

Here's to Alaska, here's to the people
Here's to the wild and here's to the free.
Here's to my life in a chosen country
Here's to Alaska and me.

I was born in a cabin on little Mulchatna
Raised in hard times but I had a good life
From the first time I flew with my father a singing
I knew that I'd wind up a bush pilot's wife

We sleep near the sound of a slow running river
And wake up most mornings to a drizzling rain
And we face every day like the first or the last one
With nothing to lose and Heaven to gain

Here's to Alaska, here's to the people
Here's to the wild and here's to the free.
Here's to my life in a chosen country
Here's to Alaska and me
Oh, here's to Alaska and me.

Alec clapped after her rendition. He understood her sentiments and felt the joy she must have experienced on moving to wildly beautiful Alaska. Alec then shared the circumstances that caused him to leave England and join the Pegasus.

Upon hearing about the death of his first wife and four-year-old daughter from a drunk driver, she commiserated, "I'm glad you remarried. Paige sounds ideal for you!"

Proudly, Alec declared, "She and her aunt are now on an excursion, keeping an eye on Irwin's fellow caterers."

Minutes later, their conversation returned to the matter at hand. Alec relayed the little information he had on the Silicon Valley caterers and promised to email her more detailed profiles. Though Alec didn't suspect Derek or Gail of having anything to do with Irwin's death, he agreed to include them in his report. She, in turn, promised to share everything she learned about Robert Irwin.

At 3:45 PM, Nicola received a call from McGrath advising that an ambulance was prepared to pick up the corpse and his personal effects. On being told, Alec notified Harold to have everything ready for the awaiting vehicle.

From the buffet, Alec escorted the deputy chief to the pier. As she was about to depart, she bid, "Find out who Mr. Irwin listed as his emergency contact or next of kin. To get his body back from the medical examiner, he or she will need to sign a release. If no one shows interest, the state will handle his corpse as an 'unclaimed remains.'"

Now eager to find Robert Irwin's contact, Alec waved goodbye to Nicola and hurried to the office he shared with his assistant, Regina Hill.

Regina welcomed Alec with a big hug but complained, "You and Paige have been back on the Pegasus for two days, and this is your first opportunity to say hello?"

Alec apologized, "I'm really sorry. Time just got away from me."

Grinning, she replied, "I guess a murder is a good reason. I'll forgive you if you tell me about your vacation in California."

Over the next twenty minutes, Alec gave her the highlights and confirmed what was happening in his latest investigation. Regina knew much of it from Douglas and asked, "So, what brings you here now? You don't have to return to work until next Tuesday."

Although Regina Hill was in her seventies, she possessed an ageless quality. She reminded Alec of one of his favorite old-time actresses, Helen Hayes, who often played the role of Agatha Christie's Miss Marple. Regina was about five feet tall and plump.

Her gray hair was arranged in a French knot that sat neatly on her head.

Getting down to the reason he was there, Alec relayed, "I need to find out who Bob Irwin listed as his emergency contact when he booked this cruise."

Before Alec could finish his request, Regina brought up the info on her computer. Alec glanced at the name and exclaimed, "Bella Valentino! I wonder why he named her. I can't imagine they were ever close. Maybe there was no one else."

Alec thanked her with a grateful smile and said, "I also promised the Deputy Chief of the Juneau Police the bios of the people who rubbed shoulders with Irwin. Since Bella is on the same excursion as Paige and her aunt, I'd better get started on that task. They won't be back until seven."

Walking to the computer on his uncluttered desk, Alec muttered, "I hope I can remember my password."

When Regina returned to the reports on her desk, she sighed, "It's good to have you back."

At six o'clock, Regina and Alec decided to call it a day. After saving what he had written on his computer, Alec suggested, "Let's get some dinner on the Lido Deck."

The pair found Douglas near his usual spot at the buffet. Before joining him, Alec collected roasted turkey and its sides from the carvery station. The doctor was keen to hear how Alec made out with Nicola Campbell, a fellow Scotsman."

Regina, nearly dropping her salad fork, exclaimed, "You didn't tell me the deputy chief was a woman, much less Scottish!"

"And lovely," Dr. Abbot added.

Alec couldn't disagree and admitted, "It was wonderful to hear her Glaswegian accent. I think we'll work well together. We have a lot in common. In fact, Nicola sang to me."

Lightheartedly, Regina warned, "You'd better not make Paige jealous."

Alec promised, "I wouldn't dare," and then asked Douglas, "What do you know about Anavar tablets? They were discovered in Robert Irwin's cabin.

The doctor explained it was a popular oral anabolic steroid and considered one of the safest pills in helping bodybuilders maintain muscle while burning calories during a cutting phase.

Alec had never heard the term "cutting" and learned from Douglas that bodybuilders usually alternated between cutting and bulking. Deciding to research it later, Alec checked his watch and excused himself.

That and other things were on his mind when Alec returned to his cabin to find it empty. On the bed was a note from Paige dated 7:10 PM, saying, "Aunt Irena is resting in her cabin. Bella and I are going to have a drink in the Ocean Bar. Come by if you can."

CHAPTER FIVE

▼

"Dreams"
Words & Music by Stevie Nicks
Genre: Soft Rock, Released: March 1976

Tuesday Evening—5th of August

Alec hurried to the Ocean Bar, eager to see his wife, spend time with Bella Valentino, and re-acquaint himself with his native beverage. Alec had been careful to stay away from Scotch while recovering from his stomach bug.

On entering the lounge, Alec was waved over by the ladies. Before joining them, Alec stopped by the bar to pick up a neat whisky.

Paige was halfway through her gin and tonic, and Bella was nursing a cosmopolitan—a vodka cocktail made with triple sec, cranberry juice, and lime. Even though the ingredients weren't exotic, the name "Cosmo" suggested that those drinking it, like Bella, were sophisticated.

Alec gathered from the two women that Aunt Irena and Nancy Lawton hit it off immediately. At the Mendenhall Glacier, Irena and Nancy were happy to admire the ice field from a bench and remain a distance away from bears that often lurked on hiking trails.

Paige and Bella were more adventurous and walked around the area before trudging up multiple steps to the hilltop information center. In the building, they watched a fifteen-minute film and learned about the glacier's geography, ecology, and history. At 3:45 PM, the bus driver took the group to the Macaulay Salmon Fish Hatchery.

Excitedly, Bella relayed in her sexy Italian accent, "It was so interesting. We learned about the salmon's life cycle. Baby salmon, called smolt, spend about three months growing and imprinting in the company's saltwater pens. They're released in late spring to early summer and spend one to six years in the ocean. Once they mature, they fight to return to where they were born."

Paige added, "We watched adult salmon amass in the bay and swim up a 450-foot fish ladder that looked more like a staircase. At times, the fish looked comical. Upon reaching their destination, the salmon are separated by species, and their fertilized eggs are placed in freshwater incubation rooms. The whole process is then repeated."

Confused, Alec asked, "What do they do with the adult fish?"

Paige laughed. "I wondered that myself and was told that once Pacific salmon release eggs and sperm in a body of water, they die. At the hatchery, the carcasses of the adult salmon are sent to processors where they are turned into a natural fertilizer."

Alec gulped, "I'm glad I'm not a male salmon."

Bella laughed and replied, "We were told that Atlantic salmon are different and can repeat the spawning cycle for several years."

Paige wisely changed the subject and interjected, "After visiting the hatchery, we were taken to Salmon Creek for a cookout. The food was ample and fine for its rustic setting. Wild salmon was grilled over an open Alderwood fire. It was served with ribs, baked beans with reindeer sausage, au gratin potatoes, coleslaw, and salad."

Bella sighed, "I was letdown. While the weather was pleasant and the salmon fresh, there were many flies. The outdoor benches were uncomfortable, and the place was crowded with tourists from other ships. The creek's waterfall was nice," and gazing at Paige, Bella added, "And the company."

Over a second round of drinks, Alec got a chance to question Bella about Bob Irwin. Unsure how she'd react, Alec broached the subject cautiously and stated, "I met with two officers from the Juneau Police Department this afternoon. They collected Mr. Irwin's body and his personal effects. They'll be sending them by seaplane to Anchorage, where the medical examiner will open an investigation and conduct an autopsy."

Though Bella's face didn't change, Alec noticed physical tension in her fingers and shoulders. He continued, "The police officers have asked me to give them the decedent's emergency contact, and I found out that Mr. Irwin named you."

This time, Alec could see shock on her face and asked, "You weren't aware he listed you as a contact?"

Swallowing a large mouthful of her cosmopolitan, Bella replied, "Bob has … been divorced for over twenty years. I believe his former wife still lives in England. After my husband passed away, he and I briefly dated. I never heard him mention other relatives. I suppose that's why he listed me."

Alec doubted it was that simple and wanted to know when she dated Bob, why they broke up, and how they recently got along. Trying to explore those issues, Alec remarked, "I heard Mr. Irwin had issues with his fellow caterers. Derek told me that he refused to let Carlos out of his contract and had reported Brett for missing a license on her food truck."

Bella nodded sadly. "Robert was his own worst enemy. He grew up with a chip on his shoulder. You wouldn't have thought it by looking at him, but Bob used to be scrawny. He was bullied as a kid while growing up in Swindon. His mother never married his dad, and he left home when he was fifteen to join the Royal Navy."

Alec realized that Bella knew more about the decedent than the other members and wondered how long they dated. Concerned she would clam up, Alec remarked, "You got to see a vulnerable side of Mr. Irwin. Was it difficult to break through his façade?"

Bella shrugged in a very Italian way and replied, "I wasn't in great shape after my husband died. Tony was only in his forties when a ruptured brain aneurysm caused his death. Bob and my husband used to visit the same health club in London. At that time, Bob was on an anabolic steroid regimen and injected them intramuscularly."

Pleased that she confirmed Irwin's drug use, Alec asked, "Why did you two break up?"

Alec could see by her pinched features that she didn't want to answer. Hesitantly, she replied, "It was a destructive relationship. We were both lonely and broken."

With that said, Bella finished her drink and rose to go. Paige thanked her for her honesty and stated, "I hope we can get together again."

Gazing at Alec, Paige added, "And we haven't upset you."

When Bella Valentino departed, the eyes of several men in the Ocean Bar followed her. She had dark eyes and hair that invited admiring glances. Although her clothes were appropriate for a day out, it was obvious that she didn't need to wear low-cut outfits to get attention. The woman had animal magnetism.

The song by Fleetwood Mac came to Alec's mind, and he sang out,

Now here you go again
You say you want your freedom
Well, who am I to keep you down?
It's only right that you should
Play the way you feel it
But listen carefully
To the sound of your loneliness

Like a heartbeat drives you mad
In the stillness of remembering what you had
And what you lost
And what you had
And what you lost

Oh, thunder only happens when it's rainin'
Players only love you when they're playin'
Say women, they will come and they will go
When the rain washes you clean, you'll know
You'll know

Now here I go again
I see the crystal vision
I keep my visions to myself
It's only me who wants to wrap around your dreams
And have you any dreams you'd like to sell
Dreams of loneliness

Like a heartbeat drives you mad
In the stillness of remembering what you had
And what you lost
And what you had
Ooh, what you lost

Thunder only happens when it's rainin'
Players only love you when they're playin'
Women, they will come, and they will go
When the rain washes you clean, you'll know

Oh, thunder only happens when it's rainin'
Players only love you when they're playin'
Say women, they will come and they will go
When the rain washes you clean, you'll know

You'll know
You will know
Oh, you'll know

Paige patted her husband's hand when he ended the song and commended, "Your timing is improving. I'm glad you waited for Bella to leave."

Alec nodded and looked at his watch. "Let's finish our drinks and call it a night. It's nine now, and we were both woken up early."

As they rose from the table, Paige reminded Alec, "The ship will be cruising Endicott Arm and Dawes Glacier tomorrow. I'm going to take it easy. My head cold has moved from my sinuses to my throat, and the phlegm is starting to irritate me."

Once back in their suite, Alec helped Paige fill the tub for her nightly bath. It took only seconds for her to disrobe and sink under the foamy bubbles. While resting her head on a rolled-up towel, she asked, "Can you make me a hot toddy? It always helps me sleep."

"Your wish is my command, Lass," Alec replied on his way to the kitchenette.

From a top shelf, Alec brought down a bottle of whisky he had squirreled away against the ship's rules. Since he only used it for hangovers and colds, Alec deemed it medicine and not alcohol.

After inserting a decaf tea bag into a mug of hot water, Alec added squeezed lemon slices, a heaping tablespoon of honey, and two ounces of whisky. It was still piping hot when Paige took it from him in the bathtub.

As she sipped the magic elixir, Alec updated Paige on his investigation and Nicola Campbell's plans. When the pair got into bed, Alec turned off the lights. While snuggling up to Paige, Alec thanked God for placing her in his life.

Seconds later, they were both fast asleep.

At 8:00 AM, the ship's loudspeaker invited passengers to amass at the ship's bow to witness its entry into Endicott Arm Fjord. Paige and Alec ignored the announcement and remained under the covers until nine. They were forced out of bed when Paige's father and aunt knocked at the door.

Their visitors arrived with a plateful of pastries, rolls, assorted fruit, and cheeses. Thrilled that they had brought breakfast, Alec ushered them in while Paige prepared coffee.

Since their guests had already eaten and wanted to hear about the latest murder, they were very attentive. Alec relayed the events from the day before. Aunt Irena added what she learned about Nancy Lawton on the excursion, mentioning they got on like a house on fire. Hoping her new friend wasn't an axe murderer, Irena acknowledged, "I'll keep my wits about me."

Paige smiled adoringly at Irena and asked, "What are you going to do today?"

Pulling the ship's activity guide from her quilted tote bag, she declared, "Your dad and I plan to put on a warm coat and go up to the bow. We'll be able to see Dawes Glacier at ten. It's over six hundred feet tall and a mile broad. You don't get to see glaciers in Maine. At least, not since the Ice Age.

"At 11:30, we plan to attend the Alaska Up Close lecture in the Starlight Lounge. The topic will be the Iditarod, the thousand-mile-long dogsled race from Anchorage and Nome."

Russell added, "We'll be on babysitting duty from 2:00 to 3:30 so that Derek and Gail can attend their ACA meeting and have afternoon tea. We spoke to them earlier, and they'd like us to meet them at the Britannia Dining Room at six-thirty tonight. Can you two make it?"

Alec agreed, "That won't be any problem. Who's going to watch Oliver?"

Irena replied, "They hope to bring him. He eats most people food now, and Gail will take him back to the cabin if he throws his meal on the floor."

Paige giggled. "I can't wait." Gazing at Alec, she resumed, "What are your plans?"

After letting her know that he needed to shower and finish the ACA member bios for Nicola Campbell, Paige responded, "In that case, I'm going to tag along with my dad and Irena. I just need to dress."

While Paige got ready, Alec cleaned the kitchenette and entertained his relatives. It was good to have family around, and Paige's nearest and dearest were easy to get along with. The same could *not* be said about his mother. She was difficult at the best of times.

Minutes later, Paige was outfitted in a puffy jacket and beanie hat. Alec couldn't help thinking she looked like the Stay-Puft Marshmallow Man. She kissed him goodbye and suggested, "Look for us at the lecture if you finish early."

Alec promised and watched them go. Once again, he was reminded of how lucky he was.

It was 11:30 AM when Alec finished collecting information on Robert Irwin and his fellow caterers. Their websites were full of specifics, and Alec located various news articles about the chefs online.

While on his computer, Alec proofread:

Bios of ACA Members
(Silicon Valley Chapter)

Robert Irwin
Owner of Irwin's Power Meals (Meal Plan)
(Website: IrwinsPowerMeals.com)
Developed Irwin's Energy Bars
(Website: IrwinsEnergyBars.com)
Moved to Santa Clara, California
Executive Chef at a neighborhood steakhouse in London
Married and divorced within five years
Settled in London, England
Worked with Claude Bourdain on FCL's Aquarius as Grill Chef
Joined the British Navy at 15 and rose to Assistant Chef
Born in Swindon, England

Bella Valentino
President of the SV chapter for three years
Owner of Bella's Bounty
(Website: BellasBountyCaterers.com)
Food host for a public TV channel
Food Critic for a local paper
Authored two best-selling cookbooks
Begin catering company
Moved to Palo Alto, California
Husband died from a brain embolism
Son born in London
Worked for a food magazine in London
Married to Anthony Valentino
Graduated from college with a journalism degree
Born in Rome, Italy

<u>Jeffrey Webber</u>
Owner of SV Corporate Caterers
(Website: SVCorporateCaterers.com)
Started and expanded catering business
Moved to Santa Clara, California, with daughter after wife's death
Wrote three "How To" books
Taught at 4-year Culinary Arts College on Long Island
Sous Chef in Manhattan restaurant
Graduated from NYC culinary college
Conducted cooking demos while at school
Born in Worcester. Massachusetts

<u>*Brett Webber (Daughter of Jeffrey)*</u>
Owner of a food truck specializing in international comfort foods
(Website: AroundtheWorldComfortFoods.com)
Food blogger
Worked as a line cook for father's catering company
Moved to Santa Clara, California, with father
Back-packed throughout Europe and Asia
Attended cooking school in New York
Born in New Hyde Park, New York

Mei Chung
Private chef for Silicon Valley CEO (family of 4)
Moved to Palo Alto, California
Executive Chef at Las Vegas restaurant
Banquet Chef at Las Vegas casino
Degree in Culinary Arts
Degree in Food and Beverage Management
Trained in all styles of cooking
Immigrated to Dearborn, Michigan, as a child
Born in Guangdong, China

Carlos Ruiz
Assistant Chef and junior partner for Irwin's Power Meals
Mentored by several prestigious chefs
Competed in culinary contests
Moved to Sunnyvale, California
Chef at Tucson bistro
Blogger and photographer of food
Graduated from culinary school
Worked at family's bed and breakfast
Born in Tucson, Arizona

Nancy Lawton
Bakes low-calorie, healthy desserts for Anderson's catering company
Moved to San Jose, California, with husband
Catered baked goods at private parties
Conducted cooking classes for adults
Judged baked goods at county fairs
Wrote two dessert cookbooks
Married Ronald Lawton and had one daughter and two sons
Worked in a test kitchen of a yogurt company, developing recipes
Studied Food and Nutrition at Buffalo State College
Sold produce and freshly baked breads at Farmer's Markets
Born in Elmira, New York, on the family farm

Derek Anderson
Owner of Deliteful Dinners and Desserts (Meal Plan)
(Website: DelitefulDinners.com)
Owner of Cupertino Caterers
(Website: CupertinoCaterers.com)
Sous Chef at Michelin-starred restaurant in San Fransico
Married Gail Martin
Assistant Food and Beverage Manager on FCL's Perseus
Degree in Hospitality Management from Univ. of California, Davis
Born in Cupertino, California

Gail Martin Anderson
Owner of Deliteful Dinners and Desserts (Meal Plan)
(Website: DelitefulDinners.com)
Owner of Cupertino Caterers
(Website: CupertinoCaterers.com)
Married Derek Anderson and later gave birth to a son
Continuing education classes in nutrition, dietetics, and food safety
Employed at Overeaters Anonymous in San Jose
Degree in Clinical Psychologist from Univ. of California, San Diego
Born in Santa Clara, California

Claude Bourdain
Senior Executive Chef on the FCL's Pegasus
Assistant Executive Chef on FCL's Cygnus
Chef de Cuisine on FCL's Aquarius
Sous Chef on the FCL's Aquarius
Junior Sous Chef on FCL's Perseus
Worked at the school's restaurant
Studied Culinary Arts at NYC college
Born in Strasbourg, France

Though Alec was confident that Derek and Gail had nothing to do with Irwin's death, he included their bios. He also added facts about Claude Bourdain that had been included in the ship's officer profiles.

The executive chef had not been happy to see Bob Irwin at his seven-course dinner. They both served on the Aquarius. Hoping to find out what they might have locked horns over, Alec composed the following email:

Subj: Information on the ACA Members, Silicon Valley Group
Date: 6th of August, 1:11:51 PM AKDT
From: AlecDunBarton@aol.com
To: NCampbell@JuneauPD.org

Deputy Chief Campbell,

It was good to meet you yesterday. I've inserted the crime scene photos, the surveillance video of the fitness center (from the start of this cruise), and the bios of Robert Irwin's fellow caterers. I looked over the camera footage to see if any of my suspects had visited the gym before Irwin's death and didn't spot them.

While informing the ACA members about Irwin's death, I let them believe it resulted from an accident or illness. None of the caterers asked if there were video cameras in the gym or whether they captured the incident. I learned that Bella Valentine was listed as Robert Irwin's emergency contact. She had a personal relationship with the deceased years ago.

Ms. Valentino initially met Robert Irwin while living in London. He had been friends with her husband, Anthony. When Tony Valentino died suddenly from a cerebral aneurysm, Bella and Irwin got together. She called it a "weak point in her life" and described their relationship as "destructive." I plan to speak to all the SV caterers over the next few days. I will share whatever I discover.

Please let me know the results of the medical examiner's autopsy. If the toxicology report indicates he was poisoned or recently injected with a foreign substance, it will affect my line of questioning. I look forward to working with you and appreciate any help you can provide.

Alec

Alec ensured all the inserts were downloaded before pressing the send icon. After logging off the computer, he set off for the Lido buffet to grab a quick lunch.

CHAPTER SIX

▼

"The Rainbow Connection"
Words & Music by Paul Williams and Kenneth Ascher
Genre: Folk Rock, Released: June 1979

Wednesday Afternoon—6th of August

Upon entering the restaurant, Alec looked for Paige and her family. Since they had probably been and gone, Alec picked up two ready-made mini sandwiches. Despite being undersized and filled with unusual ingredients, Alec finished them with a glass of unsweetened iced tea.

It was 1:50 PM when Alec stepped into the Hudson Room. Only Bella, Nancy Lawton, and Mei Chung were in attendance. Since Bella and Nancy were in the midst of a conversation, Alec took the opportunity to speak to the Chinese-born chef.

From her profile, he knew she was a private chef for a family of four and asked, "What's it like to cook for one family?"

Mei appeared shy initially. Though she lived in the US for most of her life, she replied with a sing-song accent and explained, "The family I work for entertains often. On those occasions, I have to plan, food shop, and cook for many people, sometimes over fifty. The family has two teenage boys, and they keep me busy. You can't imagine how much they and their friends eat."

Alec laughed to himself, pondering what Oliver would be like in his teens. By then, he expected most of his food would end up in his mouth. Curious whether she lived with her employer, Alec posed the question.

Mei replied, "I live in a backyard cottage on the other side of their pool. It's very private and perfect for me. Depending on my family's schedule, I work in their house five to six days a week. Sometimes, they're gone for weeks, and I housesit. At other times, I've been requested to cook on their yacht or at their vacation home in the French Riveria."

After chatting with her, Alec better understood what a private chef does. He was touched by the way Mei spoke about "her boys." She seemed to have a closer relationship with them than their parents and treasured the moments they confided in her.

Since Mei appeared to be in her mid-forties, Alec wondered whether she ever married and had children of her own. Their conversation was cut short when Bella called their meeting to order and pronounced, "I'm glad to see you all here. I'd like a few of you to share what you did in Juneau. With so many excursions available, it's unfortunate we couldn't take them all."

Jeffrey spoke first and replied, "I took the Taku Lodge, Feast & Five Glacier Seaplane Discovery Tour. I viewed snowcapped mountains, the Tongass National Forest, and the Juneau Ice Field from a floatplane. At Taku Lodge, our group was given Alderwood grilled salmon and other Alaskan cuisine. I'm not sure it was worth the 475.00 dollars I paid, but I thoroughly enjoyed the state's majestic scenery from the air."

Nancy shared which foods were served on her salmon bake, voicing that Jeffrey's meal sounded better and more intimate. Derek and Gail, who went on the Juneau Walk in Partnership with Food and Wine Magazine, had a lot to say about their outing. Despite having Oliver with them, they had a great time visiting Fisherman's Memorial and snacking on crab bisque, halibut ceviche, smoked salmon dip, spruce tip jelly, rockfish taco, craft beer, herbal tea, and a blueberry Mojito.

The caterers who went on other excursions had questions about the preparation and taste of the samples. Alec, thirsty after having a salty lunch, decided that their blueberry mojito sounded the most appealing.

Twenty minutes later, the group turned their discussion to the upcoming food trivia contest that was to be held the following day. Faith Rossi, the ship's cruise director, had asked both chapters to devise twenty-five questions to test the passenger's culinary knowledge. Once given each list, Faith planned to narrow them down to the best twenty-five.

The meeting became spirited at that point. Several people shouted out questions, and Bella had Jeffrey write them down. Carlos argued that many were too easy, and Brett Webber responded, "You can't expect the general population to know as much as us."

Alec watched the caterers as they narrowed their trivia questions to the twenty-five. The meeting ended a few minutes to three o'clock.

At its completion, Bella handed Alec the list and asked, "Would you mind giving it to Faith? We plan to try your 3:00 PM afternoon tea in the Britannia Dining Room."

Eagerly, Alec took it and promised, "I'll give it to her right away." Recalling that Derek and Gail were joining her, he called, "Don't fill up the sandwiches and scones. You won't have an appetite for dinner."

On the way to Faith's office, Alec gazed at the list and noticed how neatly it was written. Even the crossed-out questions looked tidy. Wondering whether Jeff Webber had Obsessive Compulsive Disorder, Alec knocked on the cruise director's door.

Faith welcomed Alec. Noticing the paper in his hand, she asked, "Can you stay a moment and help me select the questions for the trivia game. Thrilled to use his culinary knowledge for something other than eating, Alec watched her lay the sheets side by side and entered the best ones on a Word document.

It took a while to remove the simplest and most challenging questions. When they finished, Alec glanced at the final trivia questions and answers. It read:

1. What is the primary ingredient in the Middle Eastern dish falafel?
   Chickpeas
2. What nuts are used to make marzipan?
   Almonds
3. Which spice is derived from the Crocus flower and is one of the most expensive spices in the world?
   Saffron
4. Arachibutyrophobia is the fear of which food sticking to the roof of your mouth.
   Peanut butter
5. Which country drinks the most coffee in pounds per year?
   Finland
6. True or false: Storing guacamole with the pit prevents browning.
   False
7. What makes broth different than stock?
   Broth is made with meat, and stock is made with bones.
8. True or false: Alcohol completely evaporates during cooking.
   False
9. A tournée cut produces what shape of a vegetable?
   Small footballs
10. True or false: The seeds are the spiciest part of a pepper.
    False
11. How many tablespoons are in a cup?
    Sixteen tablespoons
12. The process of baking a pie crust before adding the filling is called what?
    Blind baking
13. True or false: Cutting steak against the grain makes it tender.
    True

14. Gaufrette potatoes are the same thing as what?
    Waffle fries
15. What is the difference between ice cream and gelato?
    Gelato has less fat and air than ice cream.
16. What is a finely chopped mixture of cooked mushroom, onion, and herbs called?
    Duxelles
17. What is the ratio of oil to vinegar in a classic vinaigrette?
    Three parts oil to one part vinegar
18. True or false: Storing fruit in a paper bag can ripen it more quickly.
    True
19. Cooking veggies until soft and translucent (but not browned) is called what?
    Sweating
20. What is the only fruit with seeds on the outside?
    Strawberries
21. What is the main ingredient in the French stew Bouillabaisse
    Seafood
22. If pasta is cooked to be firm but not hard, what is it called?
    Al dente
23. What can be done to pastry dishes to give them a golden shine?
    Egg wash
24. What is the frozen dessert made with fruit juice rather than cream called?
    Sorbet
25. Elephant ears, beaver tails, and zeppoles are nicknames for what?
    Fried dough

Faith thanked Alec for his help but warned, "I don't want to see you or yours participate in the trivia contest tomorrow night. The ACA is planning to give the winning team gift baskets containing their cookbooks and samples of gourmet foods."

Now eager to see what Paige was up to, Alec promised to be silent during the trivia game and hurried out the door. As he approached their cabin door, he heard music.

Paige shushed him when he entered the room. A tune from Gail's cell phone came on, and Alec listened as his wife sang,

Why are there so many songs about rainbows
And what's on the other side?
Rainbows are visions
But only illusions
And rainbows have nothing to hide

So we've been told and some choose to believe it
I know they're wrong, wait and see
Someday we'll find it
The rainbow connection
The lovers, the dreamers, and me

Who said that wishes would be heard and answered
When wished on the morning star?
Someone thought of that and someone believed it
And look what it's done so far

What's so amazing that keeps us stargazing?
And what do we think we might see?
Someday we'll find it
The rainbow connection
The lovers, the dreamers, and me

All of us under its spell
We know that it's probably magic

Have you been sleeping, and have you heard voices?
I've heard them calling my name
Is this the sweet sound that calls the young sailors
The voice might be one and the same

I've heard it too many times to ignore it
It's something that I'm supposed to be
Someday we'll find it
The rainbow connection

The lovers, the dreamers, and me

Someday we'll find it
The rainbow connection
The lovers, the dreamers, and me

Paige whispered, "Gail compiled a bunch of songs to help Oliver sleep. There are tunes by Kenny Logins, Simon and Garfunkel, Donovan, James Taylor, and John Lennon, among others."

Alec listened to them on the living room couch and found himself nodding off midway through Lennon's "Beautiful Boy."

He was awakened ninety minutes later when Derek and Gail came to the door. Thrilled that Paige could watch Oliver after Russell and Irena's stint, Gail thanked Paige and then commented, "I see my music also helped your grown-up boy nap."

Derek winked as Alec sat up and complimented, "That's a great mix of soft rock and folk songs.

While Derek collected the phone, Gail looked at her watch and said, "We have about an hour to get ready for dinner. Gazing at her son, she added, "I hope he'll be good at dinner. The tooth, which has been causing trouble, has finally broken through his gum."

When they departed, Alec asked, "What's tonight's dress code?"

Paige replied, "It's casual, but you should wear your black trousers and a collared shirt."

Stroking his chin, Alec added, "I'd better shave again, too."

Paige entered the bathroom while Alec applied aftershave to his cheeks and neck. She sniffed the fragrance with approval and confided, "After giving Oliver his afternoon bottle, he spit up all over me."

Alec laughed as his wife stepped into the shower and commented, "Better him than me."

The spray of the water prevented Alec from hearing her terse response.

CHAPTER SEVEN

▼

"Murder By Numbers"
Words & Music by Gordon Sumner and Andy Summers
Genre: Jazz Rock, Released: June 1983

Wednesday Evening—6th of August

At six-thirty, the DunBartons and Andersons met at the maître d's stand on the Promenade Deck. Since Derek had made dinner reservations, their party was taken directly to a table towards the front of the Britannia Dining Room.

Alec was glad to be seated away from the thunderous engine noise at the rear of the ship. The rumbling made it hard to understand soft-spoken diners.

The steward immediately fetched a highchair for Oliver, and Gail loaded the tray with baby toys and Cheerios she'd brought from home. Though less than a year old, it appeared that Oliver was already into trucks and liked to spin its wheels.

Another server handed out the menus and asked the family whether they wanted wine or a cocktail. Russell ended up ordering a bottle of red and white wine.

The menu was extensive, and Alec selected a jumbo shrimp cocktail and tangerine-glazed duck breast. Derek and Gail chose beef tenderloin Oscar for their main entrée, and Paige, her dad, and

Irena decided on pan-fried sea bass with apples. Oliver seemed momentarily happy with his breakfast cereal.

While enjoying their drinks and appetizers, Derek asked about Irwin's death. After finishing his shrimp, Alec replied, "Right now, we can't be certain how he died or who may have had a hand in it. Can you tell me more about your fellow caterers? I know very little about Carlos Ruiz."

Gail retrieved one of Oliver's trucks that had fallen on the floor and answered for Derek, "I think Carlos is the best chef among us. He's creative and not afraid to push culinary boundaries. He can be very intense and, at other times, runs around like a little kid.

"He was furious when Bob refused to let him out of his contract and had misgivings about coming on the cruise. He changed his mind last minute."

Alec wondered aloud, "With Irwin dead, will Carlos inherit his companies? They could have had a partnership agreement."

Gail and Derek didn't know, and Alec decided that Nicola would be in the best position to find out. While waiting for the next course, Alec continued to ask questions and learned that Mei Chung had a gambling problem. The money she made as a private chef often ended up in the casino's coffers. She, too, had planned to say no to the cruise.

Alec brought up the Webbers while he tried his duck. Russell replied to Alec's inquiry about Jeffrey, saying, "Paige, Irena, and I met him this morning at the Alaska Up Close lecture. I told him that I'm Derek's father."

Gazing at his son and Gail, Russell repeated, "He's fond of you and thinks you're doing a great job bringing healthy and delicious meals to the public. He had less than complimentary things to say about Irwin and felt that *his* bulking and cutting meal plans were destroying the health of up-and-coming athletes."

Delving further, Alec asked, "What is bulking and cutting? It's the second time I've heard the term."

"Before I get to that," Derek explained, "I should tell you that Bob's first entry into the food industry occurred when he joined the British Navy and then worked for Flagship Cruise Line. When

Bob joined the Aquarius, he was pretty thin. Claude Bourdain was on that same ship and told me that Irwin became obsessed with bodybuilding. He purchased anabolic steroids from the ports of call they visited.

"As he bulked up, Robert experienced 'roid' rage and was dismissed after getting into a heated argument with a passenger."

Derek paused to take a bite of his crabmeat in bearnaise sauce and resumed. "After moving to California, Irwin started two companies—a ready-made meal program and energy bars. Those bars became popular at local gyms and, a few months ago, he was asked to sign a contract to sell them nationally."

Gail interrupted, "Carlos came up with the original recipes, and it was one of the reasons he and Irwin were at loggerheads."

Alec nodded and asked again, "What is bulking and cutting?"

Derek replied, "It's a strategy to gain muscle and lose fat. During the bulking stage, bodybuilders consume a surplus of calories to gain weight and use resistance training to build muscle. They eat protein-rich foods, healthy fats, complex carbs, and drinks with 100% fruit juice."

Irena, who had been trying to entertain Oliver, remarked, "That doesn't sound dangerous to me."

Gail frowned, "It can be. To save money, Irwin used cheaper cuts of meats with high-fat content and protein powders containing unhealthy additives and heavy metals."

Russell reacted to Gail's words, nearly choking on his fish, and said, "Surely, the FDA can't be happy about that."

Derek shrugged, "The organization hasn't been able to look into all the meal kits and ready-made dinners on the market. The FDA has been more concerned with food safety and kits that include raw meats and poultry."

Getting back to Bob Irwin, Alec urged, "Tell me about the cutting stage."

Derek finished the white wine in his glass and imparted, "That phase is shorter than the bulking stage, and Irwin's meals were much like ours with good amounts of protein, reduced fats, and non-starchy veggies. The goal is to lose fat stores and retain muscle mass and strength."

With his questions answered, Alec, who disliked dieting and exercise, moaned, "I guess bodybuilders are highly motivated."

In response, Irena suggested, "Or crazy."

Over fattening desserts of dulce de leche, chocolate lava cake, coconut tarts, and strawberry rhubarb crisp with ice cream, Alec learned that everyone respected Jeffrey Webber. He had taught for many years at a famous culinary school on Long Island and was known by his fellow caterers as "uptight, with OCD-like quirks."

His daughter was totally unlike her dad and had an expansive personality. Gail whispered to Alec, "She's gay, and Jeffrey blames himself for treating her like a son when his wife died."

While spooning vanilla ice cream into Oliver's grinning mouth, Irena shook her head and declared, "Nonsense! I don't know why people tie themselves into knots over things they can't control. Sometimes, you have to accept what you're given."

Alec agreed and asked, "What do you want to do now? It's still early. We can see a comedian in the Starlight Lounge or have a nightcap in the Ocean Bar. I believe a string quartet is scheduled to play at eight o'clock.

Irena and Russell voted for the string quartet. Even though Gail would have liked to listen to soothing music, she apologized, "We'd better put Oliver to bed. He has started to rub his eyes, a sure sign he's tired and restless."

Alec watched them depart with mixed emotions. He would have loved to bring up a child with Paige. Recalling Irena's remark about acceptance, Alec acknowledged that God had put him on his current path, and he wasn't going to argue with Him.

Since Alec had just one glass of wine with his duck, he didn't feel guilty ordering his usual neat Scotch. Paige and Irena decided to try a hot rum toddy. Paige's cold was on the way out, and Irena thought it a good choice to prevent one. Russell joined Alec in having whisky.

Their drinks were served as the musicians began to play. Relaxing to the dulcet tones of two violins, a viola, and a cello, Alec closed his eyes and thought about the day. He sent Deputy Chief Campbell the requested bios and discovered more about Carlos, Mei, and Bob Irwin.

Alec was brought out of his reverie when Russell invited Jeffrey Webber to their table. The fellow was alone and a fan of the music. He greeted everyone with a tight smile, and Russell offered to buy him a drink.

Jeffrey thanked him and said ginger ale would be fine. They remained silent while the quartet performed classical selections.

When the group took its break, Alec asked Jeffrey what his fellow caterers were doing. He learned that Brett and Carlos went to the comedy show, Bella and Nancy were at the piano bar, and Mei, her usual spot, in the casino.

In response, Alec shook his head, and Jeffrey remarked, "It's a pity she hasn't been able to shake her addiction. I hope she's saved some of the windfall she received several months ago."

Alec wondered how and where her newfound wealth came from. He also discovered that Jeffrey developed a drinking problem when his wife of fifteen years died. Unable to get further details on both subjects, Alec decided to research it later.

At 9:20 PM, Alec and Paige returned to their cabin. While Paige was bathing, Alec opened his laptop to determine whether Campbell responded to his email. Thrilled to see one, Alec clicked open the message and read:

Subj: Robert Irwin's Death
Date: 6th of August, 7:05:07 PM AKDT
From: NCampbell@JuneauPD.org
To: AlecDunBarton@aol.com

Alec,

I have mixed news for you. The medical examiner has completed his autopsy and is waiting for additional toxicology results. The autopsy revealed Irwin's use of anabolic steroids had caused cardiomyopathy and liver damage.

When the barbell's shaft dropped onto Irwin's throat, it cut off his air supply and crushed his larynx. He had bruises on his arms and wrist, indicating he had tried to stop the barbell's momentum.

After testing the blood and urine, the lab technicians detected Anavar (the performance enhancement tablets we located in Irwin's cabin). They also discovered slightly elevated levels of potassium chloride in his blood and organs. Other than the health issues cited, he was in relatively good shape despite his abuse of steroids.

The ME thoroughly examined the injection site at the base of Irwin's skull. The only drugs commonly injected in that area are Botox for cervical dystonia or platelet-rich plasma to encourage hair growth. Those drugs were not in his bloodstream. Despite running many tests on the pinprick of blood at the hairline, the medical examiner only found minute traces of potassium chloride on the skin.

As you may or may not know, it's difficult for medical professionals to prove that a person died from a KCL overdose. They usually need to rely on a secondary source, such as a potassium-chloride-filled syringe beside that body. Since the human body contains natural levels of the chemical, the ME was unable to confirm that Irwin died from a KCL overdose.

The medical examiner believes that Irwin lost his grip on the barbell when he felt the needle prick the back of his neck. Although injected KCL works quickly and may have been in the decedent's system, Irwin died when the shaft of the barbell cut off his air supply.

My superiors feel that the person who injected the needle into his skin is responsible for Irwin's death. As a result, the medical examiner has called Irwin's death suspicious and unnatural.

We also examined the masking tape on the gym's video camera. The adhesive did not contain any fingerprints or DNA. Your killer must have handled it with plastic gloves. Unless you find physical evidence or someone confesses over the next week, my department will take over from you when your persons of interest leave the ship on Tuesday.

Please let me know if I can be of further assistance,

Nicola

Alec had to reread the message twice and groaned aloud, "Nicola is right. It's going to be hard to find physical evidence."

Hearing Alec from the tub, Paige called, "Is everything okay?"

Alec joined her, eager to share what he learned from Nicola's email, and pronounced, "The Pegasus is going to dock in Seattle on the twelfth. That's not much time for me to name Irwin's killer. Bob wasn't alarmed when his assailant entered the gym. If he felt threatened, he would have stopped exercising."

Paige nodded, "A woman could have done it, too. The bench press faces the ship's bow, and his back would have been away from him or her."

Alec agreed and excused himself while Paige dried off. Without delay, he replied to Nicola's email and asked:

- Was Irwin ever arrested in England or California?
- Were Irwin's businesses solvent?
- Did Irwin and Ruiz have a partnership agreement with a death clause?
- Do any of my suspects have a criminal record?
- Where did Mei Chung's monetary windfall come from? Did she win it gambling?
- Was Jeffrey Webber ever arrested for drunk driving? How did his wife die?
- Did any of my "suspects" have access to potassium chloride?

After sending it off, Alec found it difficult to relax. The lyrics of the Sting song came to mind, and he sang out,

Once that you've decided on a killing
First you make a stone of your heart
And if you find that your hands are still willing
Then you can turn a murder into art

There really isn't any need for bloodshed
You just do it with a little more finesse
If you can slip a tablet into someone's coffee
Then it avoids an awful lot of mess

Because it's murder by numbers, 1, 2, 3
It's as easy to learn as your ABC
It's murder by numbers, 1, 2, 3
It's as easy to learn as your ABC

Now if you have a taste for this experience
And you're flushed with your very first success
Then you must try a twosome or a threesome
And you'll find your conscience bothers you much less

Because murder is like anything you take to
It's a habit-forming need for more and more
You can bump off every member of your family
And anybody else you find a bore

Because it's murder by numbers, 1, 2, 3
It's as easy to learn as your ABC
It's murder by numbers, 1, 2, 3
It's as easy to learn as your ABC

Now you can join the ranks of the illustrious
In history's great dark hall of fame
All our greatest killers were industrious
At least the ones that we all know by name

But you can reach the top of your profession
If you become the leader of the land
For murder is the sport of the elected
And you don't need to lift a finger of your hand

Because it's murder by numbers, 1, 2, 3
It's as easy to learn as your ABC
Murder by numbers, 1, 2, 3
It's as easy to learn as your ABCDE

Realizing that her husband needed to think of something else,
Paige invited Alec to join her in bed. It didn't take long to get

Alec's mind off the murder and onto a pleasanter subject. By the time he fell asleep, Alec had no worries in the world.

CHAPTER EIGHT

▼

"From Russia With Love"
Words & Music by John Barry and Lionel Bart
Genre: Movie Theme Song (*From Russia With Love*),
Released: March 1963

Thursday Morning—7th of August
Alec slept soundly and woke up ready to attack the day. Paige, who had gotten up minutes earlier, walked from the kitchenette to Alec's side of the bed with a large mug of coffee.

After placing the pillows behind him so he could sit up, Alec took the elixir with a satisfied smile and asked, "Do we have anything I can eat with it?"

Impishly, Paige replied. "What kind of wife do you think I am? Coffee with nothing to nibble on?"

At that moment, the microwave beeped, and Paige removed a plate of warmed-up French toast and pork sausage links. Although his breakfast became messy when he poured maple syrup on it, Alec consumed it with only one sausage rolling off his plate.

Sitting on the edge of the bed, Paige remarked, "I spoke to Aunt Irena, and she plans to go to the Alaska Up Close lecture about the state's history at ten. They want to know if we can join them."

Alec wasn't sure. With five days left to investigate Irwin's murder, he wondered whether his time could be better spent. Upon hearing that most of Derek's fellow caterers were taking the Sitka's Food Lover's Tour at 11:30 AM, Alec decided to book two spots on the excursion *and* attend the lecture.

Still in bed, Alec used his phone to bring up the ship's intranet site. The shore excursion page showed two open seats. Grabbing both, Alec declared, "That was lucky!"

With that chore done, Alec and Paige got ready for the day and met Irena and Russell at the Starlight Lounge with time to spare.

Alec was surprised to see the auditorium fill up. He noted a few familiar faces in the audience and was pleased that Brett Webber came by to say hello. Alec induced her to sit beside him, asking, "Are you interested in Alaskan history?"

Thoughtfully, she replied, "I love the subject of comfort food. Much of it developed when families were forced to use inexpensive ingredients. Sitka was the home of Russians in the 1800s, and I hope to learn what the people ate and how they lived." Noting that her dad wasn't with her, Alec asked and discovered that he was on the Alaska Zodiac Adventure & Fin Island Lodge Excursion in Partnership with Food & Wine Magazine.

Their chat was cut short when Faith Rossi walked onto the stage. Tapping the microphone to ensure it was live, she said, "Thank you for joining me for our Alaska Up Close lecture. This morning, we'll be exploring the history of Alaska. We'll also be handing out Forty-Nine Fun Facts about the state. By the end of our presentation, you should know why forty-nine and not fifty were selected."

One of the men in the audience called out, "Alaska was the forty-ninth state to join the union."

Faith smiled and remarked, "I see we have a smart group in attendance. I hope you'll find this presentation surprising and insightful."

The lecture combined tapped video and live narration from the cruise director. Over the forty-five-minute period, Alec learned a great deal. The area was originally settled 15,000 years ago when people from Siberia crossed the Bering Land Bridge.

Russians began claiming Alaska in the 1770s to exploit the fur trade and hunt sea otters. Their first permanent settlement was established on Kodiak Island in 1784. Russians gradually expanded their presence in Alaska and sent missionaries to convert the Indigenous people to Christianity. Since they didn't have immunity to their diseases, many died from smallpox and influenza.

Sitka was settled by the Russians in 1799, and they named it Fort of Archangel Michael. Three years later, a tribe of Tlingit warriors destroyed the settlement and killed a large number of Russians. At the Battle of Sitka in October 1804, the Russians re-established the settlement and called it New Archangel. In 1808, the town was designated the capital of Russia America.

Though Alec was told many facts, the historians in the video made him feel like he was living through the period. It became more interesting when another spokesman mentioned, "In the mid-1800s, the Russians questioned whether to retain Alaska. The fur trade had dwindled, and the British said everything north of the 49th parallel belonged to them. As a result, Russia asked the US if they wanted to buy Alaska for 7.2 million dollars."

At that moment, the theme song from the James Bond movie came to Alec's lips, and he sang softly,

From Russia with love I fly to you
Much wiser since my goodbye to you
I've traveled the world to learn
I must return from Russia with love

I've seen places, faces and smiled for a moment
But oh, you haunted me so
Still my tongue-tied young pride
Would not let my love for you show in case you'd say no

To Russia I flew but there and then
I suddenly knew you'd care again
My running around is through

I fly to you from Russia with love

Paige shushed Alec and told him to listen as the historian continued, "On March 30, 1867, the United States purchased the land. It worked out to two cents per acre.

"In today's money," he added, "It would be equivalent to $144 million and 33 cents per acre. Not everyone was excited about the purchase, and the deal was dubbed 'Andrew Johnson's Polar Bear Garden' and 'Seward's Folly.' At that time, Johnson was president, and Seward, the Secretary of State."

Faith took over from the speakers in the video and narrated, "In 1880, Joe Juneau located gold in the Silver Bow Basin of Alaska. Those who criticized the purchase decided it might have been a wise investment after all.

"Between 1896 and 1904, the number of prospectors grew exponentially. Gold discoveries in the Klondike and later Nome reached Seattle and San Francisco. The miners came from all walks of life and had to trek across treacherous, icy valleys and harrowing rocky terrain. Some became wealthy, but most returned home, unable to earn a living.

"The gold rush ended as quickly as it began, and boom towns like Skagway saw their populations fall drastically. By the turn of the 20th century, commercial fishing had gained a foothold in the Aleutian Islands. Salmon canneries and salted cod packing houses opened, and the whaling industry continued to kill whales without thought to their extinction."

Faith Rossi finished the presentation by mentioning events that helped the state become what it is now. These included the growth of aviation, the completion of the Alaska highway, statehood in 1959, oil discovery in 1968, and the development of the tourist industry, which encouraged millions of cruise passengers to visit the last frontier.

As people shuffled out of the lounge, she reminded them to pick up the Forty-Nine Fun Facts about Alaska. Since it was a few minutes to eleven, Alec, Paige, and Brett had no time to dally.

They were expected to be in front of Sitka's Centennial Hall by 11:30 AM.

Irena and Russell also had to hurry. They had volunteered to babysit Oliver so that Derek and Gail could enjoy that same tour. On the way out, Alec stuffed the fun fact list into his pocket and set off for A Deck.

After Alec showed his keycard at the security kiosk with Paige and Brett, the trio disembarked the Pegasus. Two cruise liners were docked alongside the ship, and the number of passengers coming and going was mindboggling.

Alec led the way to a free shuttle bus to downtown Sitka. A posted sign let the sightseers know that Sitka was five miles away, and the trip would take ten minutes.

Though the line for the bus was long, it moved quickly. While waiting for the vehicle to fill up, Alec recalled he had the list of fun facts. After removing it from his pocket, Alec and Paige read:

Forty-Nine Fun Facts about Alaska

1. Juneau, Alaska, is the only US capital that is not accessible by car. It can only be reached by boat or plane.
2. In 1983, Alaska's four time zones were reduced to two (Alaska Standard Time Zone and Hawaii-Aleutian Time Zone).
3. Alaska is one-fifth the size of the entire lower 48 states.
4. It is the third least populated state. Wyoming is the least, followed by Vermont.
5. Because the Aleutian Islands extend to the 180° meridian of longitude, Alaska is in both the Eastern and Western Hemispheres.
6. Semisopochnoi Island, Alaska, is further west than the Hawaiian Islands.

7.   The distance between mainland Russia and mainland Alaska is about 55 miles. The stretch of water between the Russian island of Big Diomede and the US island of Little Diomede is only 2.5 miles wide. When the water freezes over in the winter, it's possible to walk from the US to Russia on the sea ice.

8.   The tallest mountain in Alaska is Denali (formerly Mount McKinley), which is 20,310 feet high.

9.   Alaska and Canada share a border that is 1,538 miles long.

10.   The flag of Alaska was designed by a fourteen-year-old boy in 1927 after winning a contest.

11.   In 1915, the temperature in Alaska reached 100°F. It was nearly broken in June 1969 when it reached 98°F.

12.   The coldest temperature was recorded on January 23, 1971, at -80°F, which is almost as cold as the average temperature on the surface of Mars.

13.   Sitka, Alaska, is the second wettest city in the US, with 173 rainy days. The first is Hilo, Hawaii, with 211 days of rain.

14.   In the winter of 1951-1952, eighty-one feet of snow fell on Thompson Pass near Valdez. It was the most recorded snow in one season.

15.   Nearly one-third of Alaska lies within the Arctic Circle.

16.   Alaska is 14.2% water with over 3 million lakes and 12,000 rivers.

17.   The Yukon River is the third-longest in the US, after the Missouri and the Mississippi.

18.   Five percent of Alaska is covered with glaciers. A glacier is a slow-moving accumulation of ice, snow, rock, sediment, and sometimes liquid water that moves down a slope or valley due to its weight and gravity.

19.   The largest glacier in Alaska is the Bering Glacier Complex/Bagley Icefield. It covers about 1,900 square miles.

20.   Ice worms (small, dark-colored insects) live on glaciers. They move through the ice using hair-like setae on their bodies and generate their own body heat to survive in sub-zero

temperatures. They can be a nuisance to hikers and release a foul odor when they die.

21. Three of the ten strongest earthquakes ever recorded in the world occurred in Alaska.

22. On Good Friday, March 27, 1964, a 9.2 magnitude earthquake rocked central Alaska. People in Texas and Florida reported movement directly from the earthquake, such as seeing their "pools jiggle."

23. Alaska has 90 active volcanoes. The most violent eruption occurred in 1912.

24. Seven of the ten largest national parks are in Alaska. Tongass National Forest in southeast Alaska is considered the largest temperate rainforest in the world.

25. People in Alaska, especially those in Fairbanks, can often see the Northern Lights (also known as the Aurora Borealis). These natural light shows are caused by solar winds interacting with the Earth's magnetic field. They can be viewed from mid-August to mid-April, from 11:30 PM to 3:30 AM.

26. Alaska is home to bears, bison, caribou, moose, muskox, reindeer, lynx, wolves, wolverines, seals, whales, and puffins. There are more caribou than people in Alaska.

27. Moose hurt more people in Alaska than bears.

28. All three species of North American bears—black, grizzly (also known as brown bears), and polar bears—live and thrive in Alaska.

29. Polar bears don't hibernate and can smell prey (often seals) from about ten miles away. They're considered marine mammals and are protected under the Marine Mammal Protection Act.

30. Kodiak brown bears are the second largest bear in the world after polar bears.

31. Only one person has been killed by a Kodiak bear in the last seventy-five years.

32. Female polar bears can mate with grizzly bears and produce grolar or pizzly bears.

33. Alaska has about 20,000 reindeer and 750,000 caribou. Caribou are larger than reindeer and are undomesticated. Domesticated reindeer were imported from Norway and Siberia in the 1890s.

34. In 1937, Congress passed the Alaska Reindeer Act, which restricted reindeer ownership to the Indigenous people of Alaska.

35. All reindeer have red noses, not just the famous one named Rudolf.

36. There are no penguins in Alaska except for the ones in the zoo. They only live in the Southern Hemisphere.

37. Alaska has more bald eagles than all the other US states combined. Before 2007, they were on the endangered species list almost everywhere except Alaska. Many of them make their home in Ketchikan.

38. Humpback whales are the most commonly seen whale in Alaska. They migrate to Alaska in the summer and return to Hawaiian waters in the winter to breed and give birth.

39. Humpback whale songs can last up to twenty minutes and be heard by other whales over long distances.

40. There is no poison ivy or poison oak in Alaska. Instead, there is cow parsnip, also known as wild celery, which grows between five to ten feet high. If you brush against it, the plant juices can react with sunlight and cause pain and blistering on the skin.

41. Alaska's population is about 734,000, of which 52 percent are men. Anchorage is the most populated city, followed by Fairbanks and Juneau.

42. The population density is 1 to 1.3 people per square mile, the lowest in all the US states. If Manhattan (in NYC) had the same population density, the borough would have only 16 residents.

43. The cost of living is high in Alaska because goods must be shipped long distances. Southwest Alaska relies on twice-weekly barges from Seattle and other locales.

44. Children in Alaska are taught survival skills at an early age. In Ketchikan, eighth graders must spend a night on an island

with a coffee can of supplies and a tarp. The kids are taught first aid, how to stay safe in the wilderness, and what plants are edible.

45. The average lifespan of an Alaskan is 79 years compared to the US average of 78.8. The state with the highest life expectancy is Hawaii at 82.3, and West Virginia has the lowest at 74.8.
46. Alaska's most common last names are Smith, Johnson, and Williams.
47. Alaska can be typed out only using letters from the middle line. No other state can say the same.
48. After the Caribbean, Alaska is the most popular cruise destination in the world. The peak season is from June to September, with fewer cruises in May and October.
49. The Alaska Highway is 1,387 miles long and connects Alaska to the contiguous US via Yukon Territory and British Columbia.

The fun facts gave Alec a birds-eye view of Alaska's geography, wildlife, and people. When the bus set off for Sitka, Alec had a greater appreciation for the state's ragged coastline and treelined mountains.

As they neared town, Alec noticed that many of the rustic, wood-framed buildings reminded him of structures he'd seen in movies of the Old West. It felt like he was being transported to the past when pioneer life was hard and straightforward.

Paige's nose was pressed against the window, and she cooed, "The town is charming. I wonder what it's like to live here throughout the year."

The bus stopped in front of Harrigan Centennial Hall. Outside the brick building, which housed a museum and information booth, was an enormous canoe and several totem pools. A number of people were assembled at one end of the plaza, holding signs with the names of various tours.

Alec, Paige, and Brett made a beeline to a young fellow with the poster "Sitka's Food Lover's Tour." While approaching him, Alec noticed Bella, Carlos, and Nancy in attendance and decided they had been on an earlier bus.

The tour guide addressed the group and said, "I'm going to pass around a tablet. Please answer all the questions about your allergies and current physical condition. On the tour, I'll tell you what ingredients were used in your samples and how the food was prepared."

Upon giving the pad to Paige, Alec whispered, "I bet the tour company has been sued in the past."

Paige agreed, and as she filled in the answers, Alec asked Nancy what tour Mei had taken. She scowled, "The Pedal and Pub Crawl. I hope she doesn't drink too much."

Alec asked, "Pedal?"

Nancy laughed, "That one puzzled me, too. Her tour group is supposed to taste craft beers and get to know the real Sitka from a fifteen-passenger bike."

Alec chuckled, picturing the Chinese-American chef cycle throughout the town. She was short, and he wondered whether her legs were long enough to reach the pedals. His musings were interrupted when Derek and Gail arrived.

Derek explained, "We missed the bus you were on. Luckily, there was another one right behind it." Upon taking the tablet from another group member, he added, "I'm glad Aunt Irena and my dad were able to take Oliver. They've been wonderful, and we think Oliver is beginning to prefer them to us."

Alec smiled half-heartedly. His daughter Emma had died four years earlier when a drunk driver killed her and her mother. His little girl would have been seven had she lived. Thankful that the painful thought had passed quickly, Alec put his arm around Paige affectionately.

Seconds later, the tour guide gathered up his group and announced, "It looks like everyone has filled out the questionnaire. My name is Ryan. We're going to board a minibus and head first to the Harbor Mountain Brewing Company to try three of its craft beers. From there, we'll visit a few other places and sample Sitka's best bites."

Their small group of twenty piled into the minibus. On the way, Ryan continued to talk and remarked, "I've lived in Sitka most of my life. I was born and went to high school here."

When they passed landmarks, Ryan shared stories about his youth and the times he got into trouble with friends. During the short drive, the occupants learned he was half Irish and half Tlinkit. His mother and her ancestors were from a tribe that settled in the area long before the Europeans. Proudly, he revealed that his wife was an archaeologist and had recently discovered human remains near the Bering Strait.

While disembarking the vehicle, Alec whispered to Paige, "I bet his holiday dinners are *very* interesting."

CHAPTER NINE

▼

"So Far Away
Words & Music by Carole King
Genre: Soft Rock, Released: March 1971

Thursday Afternoon—7th of August

At the Harbor Mountain Brewery, the Food Lover's Tour was directed to sit at its outdoor picnic tables. The temperature was mild, and the sun was out. Over the last few days, passengers were continually told that "good" weather in Alaska was rare, and summer days in the state were changeable with bouts of haze, hard rain, and bone-chilling wind.

Alec took the vacant stool beside Carlos Ruiz and said, "We're lucky the weather has been nice. Drinking beer on a cold rainy day is not my idea of a fun thing."

Carlos agreed, "I'm not much of a beer drinker at any time."

Though Alec wanted to know what beverages he liked and how they fit in with his culinary style, he didn't get a chance to ask. A laminated beer menu was placed before him, and Ryan explained, "First, we're going to taste Island Weaver. It's a light-colored pilsner and is 6.5 percent alcohol."

It took him a few minutes to distribute the small glasses and bade, "Try it. What do you think?"

Alec tasted it and made a screwed-up face. He was not alone. Paige and most of the excursion-goers had an expression of distaste on their lips.

Bella announced, "It's very hoppy with an astringent bitter flavor."

Unable to drink the remainder in his glass, Alec dumped it on the gravel ground. Many others did the same. Two other samples were given out. The brewery's Skiff Life was a bit more palatable, and the third, The Old Man Stout, was voted the best among the group.

After allowing his excursion goers to purchase beer and use the restrooms, Ryan gathered up his charges and had them return to the bus. On the drive to their next destination, Ryan announced, "We're heading back to town. At the Mean Queen restaurant, you'll taste Alaskan oysters on the half shell, spot prawns, and Salmon Creek sparkling wine."

At the eatery, Alec's eyes had to adjust to the room's darkness. Moments later, he was able to direct Paige to a high-top table of polished wood. The first sample was the raw oyster. Paige had trouble getting it down her throat and complained, "What do people see in them? They're slimy, and you have to douse them in hot sauce to give them any flavor."

Alec nodded in agreement and tried the spot prawn. It was firm and had a sweet flavor reminiscent of Maine lobster. Alec washed his prawn down with the refreshing sparkling wine. The group was invited to take seconds of the shrimp and wine, and they were finished in short order.

From the Mean Queen, Ryan had his charges follow him to a building that was part gift shop and part unadorned garage. The tour guide had everyone sit at a long rectangular table in the rustic room and stated, "Instead of having you run around Sitka, we've brought the chefs to one locale. Here, you'll be able to try six Alaskan favorites. You're in for a treat."

The bright blue cloth on the table made the place look a little less like a garage, and, at each place setting, there was a white plate, paper napkin, and cup of water. Paige was on Alec's right, and Brett to his left. Across from them were Bella, Nancy, and Carlos. At the end of the table, Derek and Gail were seated with other people from their tour.

The first three samples included macaroni and cheese with bacon bits, slices of tangy reindeer sausage, and creamy clam chowder served with sourdough bread. Next was a Russian dumpling called pelmeni, which contained ground meat and onions. It was followed with thin slices of smoked salmon. The group finished their mini meal with Alaskan blueberry compote.

Alec watched the faces of those around him and listened to their comments. Even though the mac and cheese didn't appear to be particularly Alaskan, Ryan explained that many restaurants in town served it with surimi, crab, and smoked salmon. Families also relied on the dish while waiting for biweekly food deliveries from the mainland.

The others felt the reindeer sausage tasted like spicy beef franks, and the soup, pelmeni, and salmon were delicious. Alec liked the tart flavor of the blueberry dish and felt it was a good end to the meal. Therefore, he was surprised when Ryan announced they had one more place to visit."

The group followed him down the street to the Bayview Pub, inside a mall-like structure. He pointed out an elevator and said, "It's available for those who don't want to take the steps."

Nancy and a few older women made a beeline for it and arrived on the second floor just as Alec and Paige reached the top rung. From the bar's backroom, Ryan brought out a platter of freshly fried halibut nuggets.

Despite having had a filling dessert, Alec tried the lightly battered fish. Several people wanted more, and Alec was among them. When the nuggets were gone, Ryan handed out plastic shot glasses filled with blueberry vodka. Nancy was the only one who seemed to enjoy the flavor.

After tipping Ryan for his informative tour, Alec returned to the street with Paige and Nancy. The Alaska Pure Sea Salt Company was across the road, and the dessert caterer induced the DunBartons to visit the shop with her.

They learned from Nancy that the shop's owners got their flaked salt from the crystal waters of Sitka Sound, and no chemicals were added to it. Inside the store, there were glassine bags of salt blended with flowers, fruits, spices, and seasonings. Nancy was attracted to the gift items and a big bar of salted cocoa nibs.

While paying for the chocolate bar and a bottle of Alaskan wildflower honey, Nancy shared, "I heard Emeril Lagasse and several other famous chefs only use salt from here."

Paige turned to Alec and suggested, "Maybe we should buy some."

Alec glimpsed at the offerings, picked up a four-ounce bag of fresh lemon and lime-flaked salt, and replied, "This one should be good on most dishes."

Promptly, Paige purchased it, and the trio headed to Harrigan Centennial Hall. Several people were in line to take the bus back to the cruise port. Alec got behind Bella at the end of the queue.

It took a few minutes for everyone to board the waiting bus. Alec had Paige take the empty seat beside Nancy so he could sit next to Bella. Though the president of the SV chapter seemed okay during the food tasting, she now appeared forlorn.

Gently, Alec asked Bella what was troubling her. At first, she shook her head, indicating it wasn't serious. Alec pressed, "I can tell you're going through something."

Gazing into Alec's eyes, Bella admitted, "It's been a difficult day for me. My husband Tony died twelve years ago today. He was an executive chef at a fine Italian restaurant in Marylebone. He came home after working a full day, complaining of a headache. We didn't take it seriously.

"After having a glass of wine to relax, we watched some television. I thought Tony just nodded off. When I tried to rouse him, I realized he was dead."

Alec took her hand and confessed, "I know what it's like to lose a loved one suddenly. Anniversaries, birthdays, and holidays can be especially painful."

Getting control of her emotions, she gave Alec a half-hearted smile and said, "Sometimes, his death seems so long ago and far away."

Despite Alec's best efforts to keep the song to himself, he sang out,

So far away
Doesn't anybody stay in one place anymore
It would be so fine to see your face at my door
Doesn't help to know you're just time away

Long ago I reached for you and there you stood
Holding you again could only do me good
Oh, how I wish I could
But you're so far away

One more song about moving along the highway
Can't say much of anything that's new
If I could only work this life out my way
I'd rather spend it being close to you

But you're so far away
Doesn't anybody stay in one place anymore
It would be so fine to see your face at my door
Doesn't help to know you're so far away
Yeah, you're so far away

Traveling around sure gets me down and lonely
Nothing else to do but close my mind
I sure hope the road don't come to own me
There's so many dreams I've yet to find

But you're so far away
Doesn't anybody stay in one place anymore
It would be so fine to see your face at my door
And it doesn't help to know you're so far away

Yeah, you're so far away
Hey, you're so far away

When he was finished, Alec apologized, "I'm sorry. Some words, people, and events set me off."

Bella turned to give Alec a soft kiss on his cheek and murmured, "You're very sweet. Some men I dated after Tony's death weren't as nice as you."

Alec wanted to ask whether Robert Irwin was among them but didn't get the chance. The bus stopped at the cruise port, and people rose to disembark.

While walking towards the front of the vehicle, Bella faced Alec and said, "The ACA chapters are having dinner at the Rainbow Grill this evening. I'd like you and Paige to join our table."

Happily, Alec accepted her invitation. When they went their separate ways on the Pegasus, Paige teased, "I wonder if she plans to kiss the other cheek tonight."

Alec and Paige returned to their cabin to rest before dinner. While putting away the salt they had purchased in Sitka, there was a knock on their door. In his bare feet, Alec let in Irena and Russell.

As they made themselves comfortable in the living room, Alec asked how they spent their day with Oliver. Russell regaled all the delightful antics of his grandson, and Irena declared, "Tonight, we're having supper on the Lido Deck. The chefs are going to serve grilled salmon by the pool with Alaskan side dishes. At 9:00, we plan to test our food knowledge at the trivia contest. After hanging around you guys, we think we might ace it."

Alec smiled and said, "You won't be able to compete officially. Yesterday, the cruise director and I came up with the final twenty-five questions from the ACA's fifty."

Irena winked, "We don't care. It will be fun anyway."

The conversation then turned to the DunBarton's dinner plans. Paige let them know they were invited to dine with the SV caterers at the Rainbow Grill, and Irena rejoined, "Gail isn't going to join you. She wants to take it easy tonight and tomorrow. I don't know how much rest she'll get. That little boy keeps Russell and me on our toes."

Aware that her niece had a short time to dress, Irena nudged her brother and said, "We'd better not keep them."

As Paige escorted her guests to the door, Alec headed to the bathroom to shower and shave. While the hot water was streaming down his back, Alec decided to bring up Irwin's cause of death at dinner and watch the reactions of his fellow diners.

CHAPTER TEN

▼

"Takin' Care of Business"
Words & Music by Randy Bachman
Genre: Blues Rock, Released: January 1974

Thursday Evening—7th of August

Alec and Paige arrived at the maître d's podium at 6:05 PM and were taken to a large round table set for nine. Derek, Bella, Carlos, Mei, Jeffrey, Brett, and Nancy were already seated. As usual, Bella was dressed provocatively.

Alec took the empty seat to the right of Mei and Paige to the left of Jeffrey. While the menus were handed out, the sommelier came by to take the wine orders. Bella ordered a bottle of red and white that the fellow recommended.

After the meal orders were taken, Bella asked Mei and Jeffrey about their tours in Sitka. They were the only two ACA members who hadn't taken the Food Lover's Tour. Chuckling, Mei shared some of the amusing tales she heard while visiting the town's historic sites, which included its former red-light district.

Jeffrey reported, "I was on the Alaska Zodiac Adventure and visited Fin Island Lodge. The expedition vessel was very comfortable, and the seafood served at the cabin was fresh and filling. I hope I can do justice to the meal here."

The topic then changed to the evening's food trivia game and the prizes the ACA members planned to give the contest winners. Among the cookbooks, gourmet food, and culinary gadgets, Bella reminded the group, "Robert contributed a dozen of his energy bars. Should we take them out? We don't want to be asked difficult questions."

Alec turned his attention to Carlos and posed, "How do you feel about it? I understand you worked closely with Mr. Irwin and were instrumental in creating those bars."

Carlos shrugged. "Leave them in the gift baskets. I may take over that portion of Bob's business on my return to California."

Alec was about to delve deeper when the server brought over the appetizers. As the caterers dug into theirs, Alec let the matter drop. He wanted to enjoy his jumbo lump crab cakes.

Over his entrée of New York strip steak, sauteed mushrooms, baked potato, and asparagus, Alec brought up Irwin's death. Since people were eating, Alec tried to keep the discussion light and relayed, "The medical examiner suspects that Mr. Irwin was injected with potassium chloride. He couldn't be sure it caused the barbell accident.

Alec looked around the table to see how each caterer reacted. Jeffrey's face remained bland, Brett and Carlos appeared puzzled, and Mei shook her head. Shrewdly, Bella stated, "I heard that potassium chloride can cause the heart to stop, and the drug is difficult to detect in autopsies."

Nancy divulged, "I take an 8 MEQ capsule every morning. The doctor said I was low in potassium. Is the pill dangerous? Maybe I should stop taking it."

Alec replied, "I researched it on the internet. The article said it was almost impossible for a person to die from an oral overdose of KCL. It had something to do with the stomach acids. The drug is only dangerous when intravenously injected and dosage is not strictly followed."

Nancy nodded and then exclaimed, "I wonder how difficult it would be for someone to turn a capsule's contents of potassium chloride into an injectable serum." Alec hadn't considered it and decided to speak to Dr. Abbot later.

Over dessert, the conversation returned to happier matters. Bella shared how her son was doing at culinary college, and Brett told the others about the funny things that happened to her while backpacking through Europe and Asia. Mei laughed heartily, and Alec noticed she had become much more outgoing since Irwin's death.

The dinner party ended shortly later. Since it was 7:45 PM, they agreed to meet again at the Constellation Room for the quiz. From the Rainbow Grill, Alec and Paige took the elevator to the lounge, where they could admire the ocean while digesting their meal.

Upon entering the room, the DunBartons heard Douglas and Regina beckon them to their table. As Alec and Paige made their way over to them, Douglas ordered drinks for the newcomers. Both he and Regina wanted updates on Alec's investigation.

Alec filled them in and then asked the doctor what he knew about potassium chloride. Douglas was full of information and answered, "The human body contains many minerals, including potassium. It helps with nerve function, muscle movement, and heartbeat regulation. Low potassium can cause hypokalemia, which can be serious. Dietary sources of potassium include leafy green vegetables and other fresh foods."

Nodding, Alec declared, "An article on the internet said that potassium chloride can be dangerous when injected directly into the bloodstream. Would it be difficult to convert the contents of a capsule into a serum?"

Douglas, taking a sip of his G&T, replied, "Not really. You'd have to dissolve it in distilled water and autoclave it on a liquid cycle for twenty minutes. It can be stored at room temperature.

"You know," Douglas continued, "KCL injections have been used at state executions and in places where assisted death is permitted. A fatal dose is about 15 MEQ when administered intravenously and 300 MEQ if ingested orally."

Paige exclaimed, "That's a big difference!" Turning to Alec, she suggested, "Do you think Irwin's killer viewed his death as an execution?"

Alternatively, Alec countered, "Someone may have just wanted to put him out of his misery."

The foursome continued to discuss the case and decided it would have been relatively easy for the Silicon Valley caterers to convert the commonly used capsules into a deadly potion. Their musings ended when Faith arrived and took her place at a microphone in front of the Constellation Room.

The cruise director introduced Bella and Paul, the fellow in charge of the San Fransico chapter members, and explained, "Tonight, our food trivia quiz is being hosted by the American Catering Association. They will be awarding some wonderful gift baskets. For this competition, you can be in teams of four or fewer individuals."

Alec hadn't realized how many people had entered the lounge over the last half hour. When everyone was settled with a blank quiz form and pencil, Faith announced, "I'm going to ask you twenty-five questions worth four points each. I'll repeat them twice. Write down your responses on the paper. Before you exchange them for grading, I'll repeat the questions you didn't hear or understand. Answers supplied by the ACA are final. Let's begin now."

Alec watched the competitors' faces and listened as they tried to come up with the correct responses. Paige pointed out her aunt and dad in one corner, and Alec noticed a few ACA members in the audience.

It ended all too soon. When the winning team answered twenty-three of the twenty-five questions, Bella and her co-president handed out four straw baskets containing food gifts of all kinds. The champs were thrilled with the contents, and the caterers were happy that their donations were well received.

While the commotion was dying down, Russell and Irena joined Alec's table and ordered drinks. Douglas had gotten to know Russell when Alec and Paige wed in Scotland. Though Regina and Irena had recently met, they had become fast friends.

Alec was half-listening to Irena when he received an email notification on his cell phone. Making apologies, Alec opened the message and read:

Subj: Update on the Robert Irwin Investigation
Date: 7th of August, 9:21:11 PM AKDT
From: NCampbell@JuneauPD.org
To: AlecDunBarton@aol.com

Alec,

I just got hold of Robert Irwin's partnership agreement with Carlos Ruiz. Not only does Irwin's death permit Ruiz to seek employment elsewhere, but he can now take over Irwin's business interests. Per their contract, Ruiz is the beneficiary of a $210,000.00 term insurance policy on Mr. Irwin's life. I have inserted it for you.

As to Irwin's criminal past, he was arrested while living in London for distributing over fifty, ten-milliliter vials of anabolic steroids to fellow gym members at the Landmark Spa and Health Club in Marylebone. He was fined £3,000.00 and placed on two-year probation. Later, he verbally threatened restaurant patrons who complained about his food and was given a citation and community service under the Offenses Against the Person Act (ABH). It goes without saying that Robert Irwin was fired from the eatery.

Before moving to California, Irwin took up residence in New York. He was arrested for drunk and reckless driving (he ran a car off the road during a snowstorm). The other driver, Margaret Downey, was severely injured. Irwin pleaded guilty, and the case did not go to trial. His lawyer was able to reduce Irwin's felony charge to a misdemeanor. He was jailed for 90 days, given a hefty fine, and his motor vehicle license was revoked.

In California, Irwin began a business selling protein-rich energy bars and ready-made meals containing varying amounts of protein powder. The state mandates that protein powder and other food supplements carry the following warning, "There may be trace amounts of heavy metals in plant-based protein powder label (Proposition 65)." The government flagged him for omitting it on his packaging. It was rectified, but it's unknown who lodged the original complaint.

I'm still looking into your other queries (criminal records of your other suspects, Mei Chung's monetary windfall, and how Webber's wife died). After talking to several people, I've learned that potassium chloride is easy to obtain, and many people take the prescription drug. This line of inquiry may be a dead end. I'll be in touch.

Please keep me posted.
Nicola

After perusing the email, Alec opened the insert. It read:

BUSINESS PARTNERSHIP CONTRACTUAL AGREEMENT

PARTNERS

This Business Partnership Contractual Agreement (hereinafter referred to as the **"Agreement"**) is entered into on the 1st of February (the "Effective Date"), by and between **Robert C. Irwin**, with an address of Santa Clara, CA (hereinafter referred to as the "First Partner") and **Carlos A. Ruiz** with an address of Sunnyvale, CA (hereinafter referred to as the "Second Partner") (collectively referred to as the **"Partners"**).

PARTNERSHIP PURPOSE

The Partners agree that this partnership aims:
- To create and produce ready-made meals (Irwin's Power Meals) for people who exercise regularly and are interested in eating protein-rich foods to reduce weight and improve muscle strength.
- To create and produce energy bars (Irwin's Energy Bars) for bodybuilders and those interested in maintaining energy.

TERM

The Partners agree that the partnership will begin on the date of this signing and terminate in five years.

BUSINESS LOCATION

The Partners agree that the business will be located in San Jose, CA, and any change to the location will only occur by providing an attached amendment to this Agreement signed by the Partners.

NEW PARTNERS

The Partners agree that no new partners may be added to this Agreement and partnership.

CAPITAL CONTRIBUTIONS

The Partners have contributed or will contribute to the capital of the Partnership, in cash or property or non-monetary contributions in agreed-upon value as follows:

Partner: **Robert C Irwin:**
Total Agreed Value: **$210,000.00**
- Cash: $100,000.00
- Time & Effort: Creation and maintenance with an approximate value of $50,000.00
- Equipment: Fully Equipped Commercial Kitchen, with an approximate value of $60,000.00

Partner: **Carlos A. Ruiz:**
Total Agreed Value: **$125,000.00**
- Cash: $25,000.00
- Time & Effort: Creation and production of ready-made meals and energy bars with an approximate value of $75,000.00
- Other: Delivery vehicle with approx. value of $25,000.00

INTEREST

The Partners agree that neither will pay interest on any capital payment, including additional capital contributions.

PROFITS AND LOSSES

The Partners agree that appointed accountants will determine the partnership's profits and losses at the end of every fiscal year based on the partners' capital contribution values.

BORROWING OF PARTNERSHIP INTERESTS

The Partners agree that no money will be borrowed from the business without the prior written consent of the other Partner.

FINANCIALS STATEMENTS

The Partners agree to provide a financial statement at the end of every fiscal year showing the business's income and expenses and indicating each Partner's share of the profits.

MANAGEMENT

The Partners agree that the business will be managed as follows:

- **Robert C. Irwin**: Founder, Executive Chef, Responsible for Hiring Hourly Employees (as needed)
- **Carlos A. Ruiz**: Recipe Developer, Junior Executive Chef, Oversees Meal/Power Bar Deliveries

<u>DEATH</u>

The Partners agree that in case of either partner's death, the surviving partner will be entitled to purchase the decedent's interest in the partnership through a keyman cross-purchase term insurance policy for five years. The Partners also agree that the surviving partner will be entitled to terminate this Agreement and partnership.

<u>TERMINATION</u>

The Partners agree that this Agreement and partnership may *only* be terminated with approval by both partners.

<u>AMENDMENTS</u>

The Partners agree that any amendments made to this Agreement must be in writing and signed by both Partners. As such, any amendments the Partners make will be applied to this Agreement.

<u>SEVERABILITY</u>

If a court of competent jurisdiction finds a provision of this Agreement void and/or unenforceable, the remaining provisions will continue to be enforced.

<u>GOVERNING LAW</u>

This Agreement will be governed by and construed according to the laws of California.

<u>ENTIRE AGREEMENT</u>

This Agreement is complete and, with respect to the subject matter herein, supersedes all and any prior agreements, understandings, and conditions, expressed or implied, written or oral, of any nature pertaining to the subject matter herein. The expressed terms control and supersede any course of performance and/or usage of the trade inconsistent with any of the terms herein.

<u>SIGNATURES</u>

The Partners hereby agree to the terms and conditions outlined in this Agreement, and such is demonstrated throughout their signatures below:

Robert C. Irwin
Robert C. Irwin

Carlos Ruiz
Carlos A. Ruiz

Alec had just finished reading the partnership agreement when Paige repeated, "Are you listening to me?"

Alec looked up from his phone and apologized, "Sorry. It took me longer than expected to go through Nicola's email and insert."

Swallowing a large mouthful of his Scotch, he summarized what was written in Nicola's message. His tablemates listened to every detail and had a lot to say afterward. When Russell murmured, "You'd better talk to Carlos tomorrow and take care of business," Alec sang out,

You get up every morning.
From your alarm clock's warning
Take the 8:15 into the city
There's a whistle up above
And people pushin' people shovin'
And the girls who try to look pretty
And if your train's on time
You can get to work by nine
And start your slaving job to get your pay
If you ever get annoyed
Look at me I'm self-employed
I love to work at nothing all day
And I'll be

Taking care of business (every day)
Taking care of business (every way)
I've been taking care of business (it's all mine)
Taking care of business and working overtime
Work out

If it were easy as fishin'
You could be a musician
If you could make sounds loud or mellow
Get a second-hand guitar
Chances are you'll go far
If you get in with the right bunch of fellows
People see you having fun
Just a-lying in the sun
Tell them that you like it this way
It's the work that we avoid
And we're all self-employed
We love to work at nothing all day
And we be

Taking care of business (every day)
Taking care of business (every way)
We be been taking care of business (it's all mine)
Taking care of business and working overtime

Irena winked, "There he goes again. At least he has a lovely tenor voice."

Paige and Regina agreed, and Douglas, checking his watch, announced, "It's nearly eleven. I think we'd better call it a night."

The group broke up reluctantly. When the DunBartons returned to their cabin, Paige reminded Alec, "I'm going on the Wilderness Exploration Cruise & Crab Fest Excursion tomorrow morning with my aunt and dad. What are your plans?"

Alec scowled, "I need to track down Carlos Ruiz!"

CHAPTER ELEVEN

▼

"Fly Like an Eagle"
Words & Music by Steve Miller
Genre: Rock, Released: August 1976

Friday Morning—8th of August

Despite Alec's intention to get up early and track down Carlos, he failed miserably. Paige tried to wake him before leaving for her tour. After being shaken several times, Alec turned to his side and fell back to sleep.

It was nine-thirty when Alec was finally clear-headed enough to rise. According to the clock, he just had five hours of sleep. While making a pot of coffee, someone knocked on his door.

Alec opened it and was momentarily alarmed to see Harold Zuma, the Chief of Security. With a worried expression, he asked, "Did someone else die?"

Zuma crossed over the door's threshold and replied calmly, "All the ship's passengers are safe and accounted for. I'm here on behalf of Captain Stewart. He wants to see us at 11:00 AM in his ready room. Can you tell me how your investigation is going? I don't want to go in there blind."

Before responding, Alec handed Harold a mug of coffee and had him sit in the living room. It took a while to update Zuma on the contents of the medical examiner's report and what he'd learned from his suspects.

Since time was short, they agreed to meet in half an hour. Alec needed Zuma to locate Ruiz through his keycard movements while he showered and dressed. Twenty minutes later, Alec was ready. With wet hair, Alec set off for the security office, singing,

Time keeps on slippin', slippin', slippin'
Into the future
Time keeps on slippin', slippin', slippin'
Into the future

I want to fly like an eagle
To the sea
Fly like an eagle
Let my spirit carry me
I want to fly like an eagle
Till I'm free
Oh, Lord, through the revolution

Feed the babies
Who don't have enough to eat
Shoe the children
With no shoes on their feet
House the people
Livin' in the street
Oh, oh, there's a solution

I want to fly like an eagle
To the sea
Fly like an eagle
Let my spirit carry me
I want to fly like an eagle
Till I'm free
Fly through the revolution

Time keeps on slippin', slippin', slippin'
Into the future
Time keeps on slippin', slippin', slippin'
Into the future
Time keeps on slippin', slippin', slippin'

Into the future
Time keeps on slippin', slippin', slippin'
Into the future

Breathless from hurrying, Alec sat down in Zuma's office and asked, "Were you able to locate Carlos?"

The officer nodded, "He left the ship at 7:15 AM to catch the Coastal Cruise & Oyster Farm Tour with Ocean-to-Table Tasting. The excursion is four hours long and, if Carlos doesn't go shopping afterward, should return to the ship around 11:30."

Feeling better about the caterer's whereabouts, Alec gazed at his wristwatch and advised, "Let's get going. We don't want to keep the captain waiting."

Captain Charles Stewart called, "Come," in response to their knock. After taking seats in the ready room, Stewart complained to Alec, "I had expected to hear from you before now. What's going on?"

Alec reported the results of Irwin's autopsy, the lack of physical evidence supporting a KCL overdose, and the names of the people who may have been responsible for Irwin's death. Alec could tell by Stewart's growing annoyance that he was not pleased.

He quickly added, "I've been in touch with Nicola Campbell, the Deputy Chief of the Juneau Police Department. She's been able to unearth Irwin's criminal records in London, New York, and San Francisco. She's currently delving into my suspects' pasts."

Zuma contributed, "Alec is going to interview Carlos Ruiz this afternoon. He had a partnership agreement with the decedent and can take over Irwin's lucrative business interests on his return to California."

The captain also wanted to know why Irwin's assailant wasn't seen on the fitness center's surveillance equipment. Zuma explained that one of the three cameras was put out of commission by the killer.

Appearing more irritated, the captain asked Alec about his other leads. Although Alec wasn't feeling very confident, he stated, "Robert Irwin abused anabolic steroids and exhibited 'roid rage' and poor judgment while he lived. He hurt a lot of people. I still need to find out who, among my suspects, was the most damaged by Irwin's actions. When I do, I'll be able to name his killer and hand the case to the Alaskan officials."

Charles Stewart showed the two men to the door, barely containing his ire. Before seeing them off, the captain warned, "I'll want another update by Monday afternoon."

Alec sighed when they were off the bridge and followed Zuma to his office. On checking whether Carlos had returned to the Pegasus, Harold declared, "Ruiz just paid for a drink at the Lido Bar."

Alec made a beeline for the bar and caught up with the caterer, sunning himself on a lounge chair by the pool. The sliding dome above him was open, allowing the sun to stream in and the cool air to circulate the deck.

Carlos looked up from his chair when Alec's shadow momentarily blocked the sun. Not waiting for an invitation to join him, Alec took the lounge beside him and decided to approach the subject delicately.

First, Alec asked about the excursion he had just taken. Full of enthusiasm, Carlos exclaimed. "The tour was terrific! Bella was on it, too. We were taken by van and boat to Hump Island, the only oyster and kelp-producing farm in the state. On the way to the island, we saw a few eagles, seals, and sea lions. Once there, we learned about the oyster-growing process. I must admit I don't care for those slimy critters.

Alec laughed and posed, "Did you get anything else to eat?"

Carlos shook his head and replied, "Nah. I wouldn't mind grabbing a burger and fries for lunch. Would you like to join me?"

That was music to Alec's ears since he only had coffee for breakfast. While Alec ordered the food from the outdoor food station, Carlos collected two unsweetened iced teas and obtained a free table.

Alec thoroughly enjoyed the meal. The cheeseburger was juicy, and the French fries crispy. Carlos shared which excursions his fellow ACA members took in Ketchikan and divulged, "Nancy went on a pub crawl, and poor Jeffrey was dragged to the Great Alaskan Lumberjack Show and Crab Fest by his daughter."

Wondering why Jeffrey Webber had issues letting his hair down, Alec asked. Cautiously, Carlos replied, "Brett told me he used to be fun and outgoing. When her mother died and they moved from New York to California, he became more serious and, at times, depressed. Just don't tell anyone you heard it from me."

Alec then broached the subject foremost on his mind and remarked, "I understand you had a partnership agreement with Robert Irwin that will be lucrative for you."

Instead of reacting negatively to his statement, Alec was surprised to see Carlos regale, "That bastard coerced me into signing a contract that tied me up for five years. I've gotten the last laugh. Through our cross-purchase insurance agreement, I can inherit his entire business. I used to mind paying a higher premium for *his* life insurance. Now, I'm thrilled he made me buy it."

Alec could see why and asked, "Do you want to take over the whole enterprise?"

Sipping his iced tea, Carlos answered, "I have no desire to make ready-made meals. Bob used protein powders in his bulking entrées. Plant protein powders can be dangerous and may contain high levels of BPA, mercury, cadmium, and arsenic.

"People should only ingest high-quality ingredients prepared and served attractively. I only decided to work with him when he promised to give me complete autonomy over the company's menus. Unfortunately, he did the purchasing."

Alec nodded. "So, you plan to keep the energy bar business?"

"Yes," Carlos confided, "I created the recipes, and Bob agreed to use organic ingredients in the bars. I'm proud to say they contain wholesome almonds, peanuts, nut butter, Greek yogurt, whole grains, oat bran, unrefined sugar, healthy oils, and dark chocolate. They don't have any additives or artificial coloring. It's one of the reasons a national company has offered to buy them. When I return to California, I plan to finalize the deal."

Aware that Carlos Ruiz had a good incentive to kill his business partner, Alec asked, "Did you murder Irwin?"

Lightheartedly, Ruiz replied, "I wouldn't have used potassium chloride. When I thought of poisoning him, I came up with Japanese fugu. Blowfish would have been the perfect way to kill a blowhard."

Alec couldn't help smiling and excused himself. It was just approaching 1:00 PM, and he wanted to find out what Paige had learned on her excursion.

After wandering around the ship for an hour, Alec gave up on locating his wife and returned to their cabin to check his email. Since there was nothing new from Nicola, Alec cleaned the kitchen. While washing up the coffee mugs, Paige entered the cabin laden with several shopping bags.

Upon kissing Alec, she showed him her purchases—glacier-silt soap for herself, a pouch of blueberry-flavored pipe tobacco for him, and a stuffed moose toy for Oliver. As Paige changed into lighter clothes, she said, "I'm going to meet Aunt Irena and my dad for afternoon tea in the Britannia Dining Room. Do you want to join us?"

Eagerly, Alec accepted and tried to get Paige to tell him about her excursion. Paige refused, promising, "I'll tell you everything when we're all together. Aunt Irena will also want to share what she learned about Mei Chung."

By the time they departed, Alec's patience had worn thin. He was glad to see Irena and Russell in line for the dining room and tried to get them to talk as they were being led to their table.

Paige scolded, "Let us catch our breath."

Irena winked, "I suppose he wants to know what Mei told me in confidence."

Exasperated now, "Alec pleaded, "Spill, please!"

Irena waited while the server poured hot tea into their delicate porcelain cups. When he was out of hearing range, she whispered,

"Mei made a large sum of money when her employer's publicly traded company merged with another business. She bought a bunch of stocks before it was officially announced and has been terrified that the Securities and Exchange Commission is on to her."

Taking a curried tuna finger sandwich from the bottom of the three-tied plate, Alec smiled like a Cheshire cat. After choosing a mini cheese quiche, Russell acknowledged, "I know insider trading is against the law, but I'd hate to see her go to jail for it."

"Martha Stewart," Irena chimed in, "went to prison for five months. I don't understand why she took the chance. She was very successful then and didn't need the money."

"She rebounded nicely," Alec admitted. "Martha Stewart is more popular now than when she prematurely sold stocks that were going to lose value. She netted about fifty thousand dollars in profit." Responding to Irena, Alec added, "You're right. It wasn't worth it."

Paige sighed. "Nancy told me that Mei has a gambling problem and just wanted to build a nest egg."

"Whatever the reason," Alec replied, "I'll have to speak to her. I wonder if Irwin knew about it and Mei killed him before he could report her."

Over the next twenty minutes, Alec heard about the threesome's excursion. Full of passion, Irena relayed, "Our tour guide, Ethan, was a sweet young man. On the bus to George Inlet Lodge, he told us about totem poles, the local wildlife, and the Alaskan people. Highschoolers have to go on survival training. And when a Walmart was built five miles from town, everything was sold out on the first day."

Russell encouraged, "Tell them about the boat trip and the delicious Dungeness crab we had for lunch."

Finishing the last scone, Irena complained, "I'm getting there."

While she was describing how Ethan collected a crab pot from the bay, Alec noticed Bella at a table for two. She was with a gentleman whose back faced him. Her expression showed warmth as they talked, and Alec watched him place his hand over hers.

Paige, noticing that Alec was no longer listening, brought his attention back to Aunt Irena. Even though he heard her say that Ethan made the crab sleepy by rocking it like a baby, his eyes remained on Bella's beau.

When the fellow followed her out of the dining room, Alec exclaimed, "Well, I'll be! The man with Bella is our executive chef, Claude Bourdain!"

CHAPTER TWELVE

▼

"We May Never Pass This Way Again"
Words & Music by Darrell Crofts and Jimmy Seals
Genre: Soft Rock, Released: September 1973

Friday Evening—8th of August

Before leaving the Britannia Dining Room, the group made plans to meet at seven for a late meal at the buffet. Alec was acutely aware he had only four days to find Irwin's killer.

While Paige was relaxing in their cabin, Alec called Zuma to find out where Bella last used her keycard. Luckily, Harold was in his office and relayed that she'd recently purchased a cocktail in the Constellation Room.

Wanting to chat with her, Alec brushed his lips against Paige's brow and promised, "I'll meet you at the restaurant. I need to find out how long Bella and Claude have been together and whether it had a bearing on Irwin's death."

As Alec walked to their door, Paige laughed and called, "Let me know if she's still interested in kissing you."

Alec got impatient while waiting for the elevator to arrive and took the staircase to the Observation Deck. He was winded when he entered the Constellation Room and looked around the lounge for his quarry.

Unable to spot her, Alec decided to wait and took a vacant chair facing the ocean. He was, therefore, delighted when Bella tapped him on the shoulder and took the empty lounge beside him. Noting that he didn't have a drink and she wanted a refill, Bella ordered beverages from a passing waiter.

When their drinks arrived, Alec asked Bella about her catering business and what it entailed. He wanted her to feel comfortable before delving into her love life. She had no problem obliging Alec and said, "Before I get to my food philosophy, I must tell you a few things. I grew up in Rome, and my grandmother taught me to cook and handle food like it was a lover."

Alec chuckled, and Bella divulged, "My grandmama was not one of those dowdy women with baggy clothes and wrinkles. She taught me how to apply makeup and show off my assets. She had many lovers while my grandfather was alive. It's the only thing I did not try to emulate. I was never unfaithful to Tony."

With a sigh, she continued, "I met Tony in London while I was going to college, and he was working as a sous chef in Marylebone. I majored in journalism and photography and got my dream job working for a food and wine magazine. We had a son, and my life was idyllic until Tony died.

"It was Robert who convinced me to relocate. He and Tony met at a health club, and when my husband passed away, Bob showed excessive interest in me. I mistook his attention for something else, and I'm ashamed to say I gave him money and my body."

Alec nearly blushed from her turn of phrase and listened as she added, "It was short-lived, and I took his advice to start over somewhere new. Since he planned to move to New York, I chose the other side of the country and set out for California."

Finally getting to her catering company, Bella admitted, "Everything I went through has contributed to my culinary philosophy and how I present food. I started Bella's Bounty to bring beautiful-looking meals to harried homemakers, business people, and fussy singles.

"Initially, my menu was limited, and I served finger foods at engagement parties and baby showers. Word of mouth brought me more business. Today, I cater all kinds of events and use the finest and freshest ingredients. I want my food to delight my clientele's eyes and palettes."

Bella then described some dishes from her extensive catering menu. They made Alec's mouth water. Almost forgetting why he wanted to speak to her, Alec remarked, "I saw you with Claude Bourdain at afternoon tea. I was wondering how long you've been dating."

Alec waited for Bella's benign expression to become hostile. Instead, she giggled like a schoolgirl and replied, "We met six months ago when I was asked to interview him for a local public television channel. He was very kind and allowed me to ask in-depth questions about his cooking philosophy. That night, we had dinner together. And over a glorious month, we grew close. It was right before he transferred to the Pegasus.

"Neither of us was ready to end our relationship. I agreed to rejoin Claude on the Pegasus with the San Fransico and Silicon Valley ACA members. Wistfully, she added, "I had been pretty lonely and needed a good-hearted man to hold and kiss again."

Alec smiled. "I'm glad you've found that person."

Without realizing it, Alec launched into song,

Life, so they say, is but a game
And they let it slip away
Love, like the autumn sun
Should be dyin', but it's only just begun

Like the twilight in the road up ahead
They don't see just where we're goin'
And all the secrets in the universe

Whisper in our ears
And all the years

Will come and go
Take us up, always up
We may never pass this way again
We may never pass this way again
We may never pass this way again

Dreams, so they say, are for the fools
And they let 'em drift away
Peace, like the silent dove
Should be flyin', but it's only just begun

Like Columbus in the olden days
We must gather all our courage
Sail our ships out on the open sea

Cast away our fears
And all the years will come and go
Take us up, always up

We may never pass this way again
We may never pass this way again
We may never pass this way again

So, I wanna laugh while the laughin' is easy
I wanna cry if it makes it worthwhile
I may never pass this way again
That's why I want it with you

'Cause you make me feel
Like I'm more than a friend
Like I'm the journey
And you're the journey's end
I may never pass this way again
That's why I want it with you, baby

We may never pass this way again
We may never pass this way again
We may never pass this way again
We may never pass this way again

This was the second time Alec found himself serenading the lovely caterer. Like the last time, she planted a kiss on his cheek.

The two separated minutes later—Bella to meet Jeffrey Webber in the dining room and Alec to join Paige and her family at the Lido buffet. Since Alec was early, he waited for them by the restaurant's entrance.

Glad to see him, Paige teased, "It's a good thing you didn't make me track you down to Bella's abode."

Alec pointed to the cheek that was just kissed for a second time and bragged, "I'm never going to wash it again."

Overhearing them, Irena mused, "It's so nice to be young."

Since Paige also expected her brother, Gail, and Oliver to eat with them, she led her aunt and father to a large round table and asked a server to rustle up a highchair.

Paige held down the fort so her hungry relatives and husband could pick up their dinners from the various food stations. Derek, Gail, and Oliver arrived just as Alec returned with a thick slice of roast beef, Yorkshire pudding, and mushy peas.

Upon seeing Alec's savory pudding, which resembled American popovers, Gail declared, "I'm getting that. It was the only thing I could eat on our last cruise when I was pregnant with Oliver."

When they departed, Alec was left alone to entertain Oliver. To keep the lad from crying, Alec had to make funny faces. He was relieved when the others returned. Oliver was given an apple slice to gnaw on and, within moments, had little bits of it in his hair.

Everyone had plenty to say at dinner. Even though Derek and Gail hadn't booked an excursion, they were able to visit shops in Ketchikan with Oliver. Russell and Irena shared the highlights of their trip and what was discussed earlier at afternoon tea.

While having a bowl of chocolate chip ice cream, Alec brought up Bella's name. His in-laws were surprised to hear that she was seeing Claude Bourdain. After Alec's words sank in, Derek acknowledged, "I saw a man leave her cabin the other morning. I had assumed it was her room steward."

Gail added, "She was very friendly with the executive chef when we dined with him in the Culinary Arts Center. Now, I understand why she was adamant about sailing on the Pegasus."

Alec asked them to keep it a secret and posed, "What do you know about Mei's gambling problem?"

Derek replied, "We think she got hooked on games of chance while working in Las Vegas. Her life in China was hard, and she viewed the US as the land of opportunity."

Alec nodded and disclosed, "People with a gambling addiction often do it to cope with stress. The momentary high from making money replaces their anxiety and negative self-image. Others get so caught up in winning, they refuse to let anyone or anything get in their way. What description fits Mei the best?"

Gazing at Gail, Derek revealed, "Mei is aware of the mess it's caused in her life. She joined Gamblers Anonymous when one of her employer's sons found a bunch of lottery tickets in her home. When he took an interest in getting his own scratch-offs, Mei realized she was setting a bad example."

Gail and Derek couldn't stay long. It was well past Oliver's bedtime. While they prepared to depart, Alec asked, "Do you know where I might find Mei this evening?"

Derek suggested, "Try the casino first. If she's not there, she might be with Nancy Lawton. They like to listen to old-time rock and roll music."

Irena and Russell excused themselves shortly afterward. Alone with Paige, Alec suggested, "Let's find out if Mei Chung is gambling her life's savings away."

After checking the casino, the DunBartons followed the 70s music to the piano bar. They got there just as the artists finished their medley and rose to take a fifteen-minute break. Some of the audience took the opportunity to find another source of entertainment, leaving two empty chairs beside Nancy and Mei.

Both women seemed pleased when Alec and Paige joined him. Aware they'd have a short time to talk, Alec asked Mei, "Can I speak to you privately?"

Mei shrugged, "You can, but I know why you're here. Nancy knows all about my troubles."

Taking a sip from her drink, Nancy confessed, "I have just as much to lose. I helped Mei buy stock in her employer's company before it merged. We did it on E-Trade. She was afraid to use her name, so we opened the account under mine. That happened four months ago.

Alec delved, "You knew it was illegal?"

Blushing, Nancy admitted, "I did."

Paige whispered, "You weren't afraid of getting prosecuted for insider trading?"

Nancy shook her head in response and protested, "Politicians in our government do it all the time and don't get arrested."

Alec silently agreed but asked Mei, "Did you make money?"

"Not as much as I'd hoped," she reported. "After the trade settled, I got cold feet and pulled out half the profit. Nancy did some research about how insider traders get caught. They invest large amounts of money and get out quickly. The SEC uses some mathematical analysis to find them. We think I may be safe now."

Recalling that Mei seemed depressed earlier on the cruise, Alec asked what caused her mood to change. Nancy replied with a scornful expression, "Bob overheard us talk about her stock sale the day before he died. He threatened to alert the SEC if Mei didn't give him money. He was a horrid, horrid man."

To Mei, Alec probed, "Did you agree to pay the blackmail?"

"I did," she confirmed, "and told him he'd have to wait till we returned to California. It's a good thing that someone killed him."

Since it looked like the musicians were about to start another set, Alec hurriedly asked, "Why did you share your story with Irena Anderson? You must have known she was going to tell us."

Nancy smiled, "I've gotten to know Irena over the last few days, and she said you were a fair man. Are you going to report us to the government?"

Alec gazed at Paige before replying, "I'll keep it to myself as long as neither of you murdered Irwin. If you did, insider trading will be the least of your worries."

They seemed satisfied with Alec's response. As the DunBarton's rose to leave, the piano players aptly sang the lyrics to "The Gambler."

Paige refused to discuss Mei or Nancy until they were back in their cabin and she was submersed in a hot bath. Once comfortably settled, she sighed with contentment and invited Alec to join her in the bathroom.

Sitting on the tub's edge, Alec asked, "Why do you think they confessed to us?"

Paige paused before replying. "It's possible they admitted to a lesser crime so that you wouldn't suspect them of a major one."

Alec considered her remark and posed, "I wonder what motivated Nancy to help Mei do something so illegal. I need to know more about Lawton and how, if any, she hoped to stop Chung from gambling."

After bathing, Paige got into a silky nightgown while Alec turned down the covers. When they got into bed and shut off the lights, Alec found it hard to get comfortable. Sensing that Alec was restless, Paige whispered, "I've heard that some activities are better than others in making a person sleepy."

Knowing which activity she meant, Alec kissed his wife and listened as she sighed again with pleasure.

CHAPTER THIRTEEN

"Undun"

Words & Music by Randy Bachman
Genre: Rock, Released: July 1969

Saturday Morning—9th of August

The scent of a steamy hot coffee awakened Alec. Paige had just placed his oversized mug on the bedside table with a stack of pancakes she had gotten from the Lido buffet. As Alec dug into his breakfast in bed, Paige remarked, "I ran into Faith Rossi up there. She wants to talk to you and will be in her office most of the morning."

Alec found Paige's remark interesting and wondered what the cruise director had to say to him. With his curiosity piqued, Alec finished his breakfast quickly and jumped into the shower.

Paige was tidying up when he emerged from the bathroom and asked, "So, what are your plans today?"

She laughed, "I'm on babysitting duty. Derek and Gail booked a trolley ride on Prince Rupert Island. Over ninety minutes, they'll see the Canadian town and snack on Bannocks, skewered Mediterranean kabobs, and fish bites."

Alec smiled, "I wonder if Canadian Bannocks are anything like the ones we have in Scotland." Suddenly homesick for the scone-like delicacy, Alec added, "My parents have been asking for us to visit them."

Though Alec's mother was often demanding, Paige replied, "We can see them on our next vacation break."

Realizing that Paige was making a great sacrifice, Alec finished dressing and kissed his wife's cheek before heading out the door.

The last thing Alec heard was Paige's sigh. This time, it was expressing displeasure.

On the way to the cruise director's office, Alec decided it was probably over some accounting matter. As he took the offered chair in front of her desk, she divulged, "I need to tell you about my past before you hear of it through the ship's grapevine."

Taking a deep breath, she uttered, "Claude Bourdain and I were once engaged to be married. I understand he might be among your suspects."

Alec knew she and Zuma were once intimate and asked, "Was it before or after Harold?"

Faith responded, "It happened a long time ago when he was a sous chef on the Aquarius."

"So," Alec queried, "You were also familiar with Robert Irwin?"

The cruise director shook her head and said, "Bob was a bully then. I was thrilled when FCL forced him to leave the ship. He ruined my relationship with Claude and, to this day, I've held him responsible."

Over the next hour, Alec learned more about Claude, Faith, and Robert Irwin. Faith explained that Claude and Bob never got along. Claude had been brought up by a loving family in France and was allowed to go to culinary school and learn from the best.

Robert had a terrible upbringing. His father abandoned the family when he was very young, and he joined the British Navy at fifteen to escape his home life. As a young man, Robert was scrawny and picked on by his contemporaries. As a naval chef, he wasn't encouraged to be creative with food. It had to be plentiful and filling."

Faith recalled, "I was very much in love with Claude. Even though he was ambitious, he always made time for me. He took great joy in improving my palette, and we decided to move up in the cruise line hierarchy together."

Hoping to get to the cause of their breakup, Alec encouraged her to go on. Awkwardly, Faith continued, "Robert had started to take anabolic steroids while on the Aquarius. He spent a lot of time in the gym and was chastised for being less focused on work. In a matter of months, everyone noticed a physical change in him. The comments encouraged him to take more drugs and exercise harder.

"One night, I got together with Bob and a few other crew members. We had too much to drink. When the others returned to their cabins, Bob tried it on with me. He was so forceful, and instead of fighting him off, I let him do what he wanted. Claude walked in on us and reacted as you might expect.

"He listened to my explanation with a blank stare and just couldn't find a way to forgive me. Robert never admitted to being the aggressor, and I blamed myself for not fighting him off."

Alec commiserated and asked, "Did you ever tell security?"

Helplessly, Faith shrugged, "Not until he argued with several passengers and was about to be fired."

Alec thanked the cruise director for her honesty and inquired, "What's your current relationship with Bourdain like?"

Faith smiled, "It's much better now, and we've become good friends. He told me he's been seeing that sexy caterer who's on this cruise. I don't know where their relationship can lead if he remains on the Pegasus. But she has more in common with him than I ever did."

Before departing, Alec asked, "How did you feel when you saw Bob Irwin on the ship ?"

Faith replied grimly. "I didn't know he was with the catering group. If I had, I might have tried to kill him!"

Alec found her remark significant and wondered whether Faith could have placed the masking tape on the fitness center's camera. As he closed the door of her office behind him, he sang,

She's come undone
She didn't know what she was headed for
And when I found what she was headed for
It was too late

She's come undone
She found a mountain that was far too high
And when she found out she couldn't fly
It was too late

It's too late
She's gone too far
She's lost the sun

She's come undone
She wanted truth, but all she got was lies
Came the time to realize
And it was too late

She's come undone
She didn't know what she was headed for
And when I found what she was headed for
Mama, it was too late

It's too late
She's gone too far
She's lost the sun
She's come undone
No-na-na, no-na-na, no-na-na

Too many mountains and not enough stairs to climb
Too many churches and not enough truth
Too many people and not enough eyes to see
Too many lives to lead and not enough time

It's too late
She's gone too far

She's lost the sun
She's come undone

It's too late
She's gone too far
She's lost the sun
She's come undone

Though the lyrics were about life's challenges and hardships that could lead an individual astray, Alec didn't think Faith had a strong enough motive to kill Irwin. The event had happened ages ago. Now eager to check his computer for an update from Nicola, Alec returned to his cabin.

Paige was on the floor, crawling behind Oliver. Seeing Alec in the doorway, she looked up and complained, "I can't find his binky."

Recalling that a binky was a pacifier, Alec helped her look for it. They found it in Oliver's overall cuff and promptly put it back in his mouth. Carrying him to their bed, Paige announced, "He's either getting heavier or I'm weaker."

After being placed between two pillows, Oliver yawned and closed his eyes. While Paige covered him with his baby blanket, Alec opened his computer and nearly awakened the lad when he spotted Nicola's email in his inbox.

The message read:

Subj: More Info
Date: 9th of August, 9:21:11 AM AKDT
From: NCampbell@JuneauPD.org
To: AlecDunBarton@aol.com

Alec,

I spoke to a contact of mine in San Francisco and have obtained more information for you. Here goes.

Bella Valentino came up clean in both England and California. In her hometown of Palo Alto, she made several complaints at her local police station, stating she was being stalked. It occurred two years ago after conducting one of her television interviews on PBS. Ms. Valentino noticed a tall man going through her garbage. On her Bella's Bounty website, under comments, an individual left remarks about her beauty and sex appeal, which were promptly removed.

The police couldn't do much until Ms. Valentino saw that person in his car. With the license plate number, the police located the assailant and brought him in for questioning. They did not have enough to charge him, and the stalking stopped shortly later.

Mei Chung was found drunk and disorderly several years ago in a private card room. In California, card rooms are legal and exempt from state gambling laws. To participate, people must be members and can only play poker, blackjack, and other card games. After spending the night in the drunk tank, Ms. Chung was banned from the members-only establishment. Since then, she's been clean.

I couldn't find anything recent on Carlos Ruiz. He had a sealed juvenile record in Arizona that was expunged. His offense was probably not serious, but I'll try to get further info on it.

Californian authorities had nothing on Jeffrey Webber. While living in New York, he was arrested for drunk driving. Because of extenuating circumstances, he was fined a small sum and instructed to get mental health help. Shortly after fulfilling those terms, he relocated to California with his daughter.

Brett Webber got into trouble with the law over her food truck business. She obtained all the necessary food service permits from the California State Health Department and took the mandated food handling and worker safety courses. When she didn't acquire a fire safety certificate, Robert Irwin reported her. Brett's business was put on hold while waiting for the local fire department to inspect and approve the food truck's cooking equipment.

Nancy Lawton had no criminal record. To the contrary, she's been given awards by her local police department for helping the officers conduct community outreach and kids' school programs. She has also donated large amounts of baked goods at police functions.

That leaves your in-laws, Derek and Gail Anderson. Gail was arrested in 1999 for demonstrating in front of a Food and Drug Administration building in Stockton, California. She and a group of fellow dieticians got rowdy trying to prevent the FDA from regulating genetically modified food.

I couldn't find anything on Claude Bourdain. You might want to check with your company's human resource department.

I hope this helps,
Nicola

Alec reread the email twice before letting Paige take a look at it. She chuckled upon seeing her sister-in-law's name and shared, "Gail has always been a stickler about healthy food. It bothered her when Irwin added subpar protein powders to his ready-made meals."

Hoping Gail had nothing to do with the bodybuilder's death, Alec changed the subject and mused, "If Nancy Lawton is such a goody two shoes, why did she let Mei get involved in insider trading?"

Paige offered, "She may have known Mei was hellbent on doing it and wanted to prevent her from getting into real trouble. I was told that Nancy always accompanies Mei to her Gamblers Anonymous meetings and has been helping her put away money for retirement. On the ship, they're sharing a cabin."

Alec wasn't aware of how much Nancy was doing for Mei and wondered whether Ms. Lawton, as a philanthropist, killed Robert Irwin as a public service. Several states were infamous for using potassium chloride to execute their prisoners.

The pair discussed what Bella may have gone through with her stalker and possible reasons why Jeffrey Webber was mandated to get mental health help. Upon sharing what Faith had told him, Alec declared, "I'd better see Regina and ask her to contact HR. She'll be able to get info on Irwin, along with Faith and Claude."

Paige agreed and relayed, "Derek and Gail should return soon to take Oliver off my hands. I plan to invite them for drinks at five and dinner in the Britannia Room afterward. Tonight, we're supposed to dress up, and tomorrow is our last sea day."

"That sounds grand, Lass," Alec replied.

As Alec was about to leave, Paige reminded, "It's one-thirty now. Be back here by 4:00 PM to get ready."

Alec made a beeline to his office, impatient to find his assistant controller. He located her just as she and Douglas were about to step out for lunch. After turning off her computer, Regina invited Alec to join them."

Without much deliberation, Alec grinned, "I would love to. It will give me a chance to update you on my investigation."

Together, the threesome found a vacant table inside the buffet restaurant. Unlike the previous day, the weather was seasonable with a cool rain.

When everyone returned to the table, Alec tasted his stir fry and launched into his report. He hadn't realized how much had happened since Thursday evening when the food trivia contest was held in the Constellation Room. It was just two nights ago.

In those forty-eight hours, Alec:

- Conversed with Captain Stewart and promised to update him by Monday on the murder.
- Confirmed that Carlos Ruiz knew about the death clause in the partnership agreement and planned to keep the energy bar business.
- Learned about Irwin's past relationship with Bella and her deceased husband, Anthony.
- Verified that Bella Valentino has been dating Claude Bourdain for six months.
- Discovered that Nancy Lawton helped Mei Chung buy stock using insider information and was being blackmailed over it.
- Informed that Faith Rossi was engaged to Claude Bourdain when they both worked on the Aquarius.
- Ascertained that Faith was sexually abused by Bob while in a drunken state, and it caused Claude to break off his engagement with her.

Alec completed his rundown by reading the email he had received from Nicola Campbell. Although Alec hadn't planned to take a two-hour lunch, he stayed to listen to the sage opinions of his friends.

When the trio broke up, Regina promised, "I'll contact my sources at human resources right away and get the dope on Robert Irwin, Faith Rossi, and Claude Bourdain. I'll let you know when I get a reply."

Thankful for their input, Alec returned to his cabin to prepare for dinner.

CHAPTER FOURTEEN

▼

"Home"
Words and Music by Michael Bublé,
Alan Change, and Amy Foster-Gillies
Genre: Pop, Released: January 2005

Saturday Afternoon—9th of August

At four o'clock, Paige welcomed her husband and praised him for his punctuality. While he shaved, Paige shampooed her hair in the shower and called out, "Gail picked up Oliver at one-thirty. She and Derek had fun on Prince Rupert Island. Derek thinks he's getting my cold and plans to stay in tonight. Dad and Aunt Irena are going to have drinks with us, and Gail will join us for dinner at six."

Hearing every other word, Alec got the gist and stepped into the shower before she could turn off the taps. As their bodies passed each other, Alec winked, "We should do this more often."

Drying off, Paige impishly replied, "Promises, promises."

Upon entering their bedroom, Alec asked Paige what to wear.

Taking her eyes off her makeup mirror for a second, she pointed to dark trousers, a white shirt, and a tie lying on the bed.

Alec dressed quickly and watched his wife with admiration while she donned a royal blue gown that had a slit up one side. The outfit set off Paige's short, strawberry-blonde hair. Realizing he was a lucky man for the umpteenth time, Alec escorted his wife to the Ocean Bar.

Irena and Russell were seated in the bar's alcove when the DunBartons entered the lounge. The quartet was performing a selection from Haydn's Opus 76. Quietly, Alec and Paige took their seats and summoned a server to take their drink orders.

While Alec was waiting for their beverages, Jeffrey entered the lounge. The caterer joined them with a thankful expression. The bar's occupants were silent for the remainder of the quartet's presentation.

When the musicians finished their set, Alec asked Jeffrey why he received a light sentence for drunk driving. Paige gave Alec a look that said, "Maybe you shouldn't do this now."

Jeffrey didn't seem to mind and replied, "I mixed pills and alcohol shortly after hearing about my wife's death. I wasn't thinking straight. Peggy was everything to me. She was a pastry arts instructor at the same culinary college where I taught. I must admit I still miss her. She would have been much better with Brett."

Alec was aware that his daughter was a lesbian and that women chefs often had a hard time breaking into the food industry. Uncertain about what Jeffrey was referring to, Alec probed further and learned that Brett had a poor self-image over her weight.

With a half-hearted smile, Jeffrey admitted, "My daughter was fourteen when Peggy passed away, and she became fixated on food shortly afterward. Her food truck not only serves American comfort foods but also those from all over the world. She makes English shepherd's pie, Egyptian falafels, Greek moussaka, and Indian samosas. That's only to mention a few."

Alec's hunger pangs increased while Jeffrey talked about her more exotic dishes. Proudly, he exclaimed, "Her food truck business is doing well. She worked hard to get it going. Bella lent her money to buy a second-hand truck, and everyone, except Robert Irwin, encouraged her."

Glad that his name came up, Alec asked, "Is it true he reported Brett over a fire inspection certificate?"

Jeffrey nodded. "That man couldn't stand to see anyone but himself get ahead."

Noting it was a few minutes to six, Alec invited Jeffrey to have dinner with them in the Britania Dining Room. Before Webber could reply, Gail showed up with Brett in tow and said, "Look who's coming to dinner."

Jeffrey smiled at his daughter and said, "It will be nice to have her with us. Brett likes the jarring sights and sounds in the Lido buffet, while I prefer the restful atmosphere in the dining room."

Brett laughed, "My dad is a fuddy-duddy."

As the group rose to leave, Irena complimented Brett. She was dressed up for the gala evening, wearing black slacks and a glittery silver top. Irena received a grateful smile from her, and Alec realized he knew little about Brett and even less about their father-daughter relationship.

The line for the dining room was longer than usual. Glad that Paige had made reservations, Alec went up to the right side of the kiosk and said, "We booked for five but now have a party of seven."

The fellow helping the maître d' replied, "That's not a problem," and alerted one of the waitstaff to take them to a large round table in the middle of the restaurant. Alec helped Brett to her seat and took the one beside her. Once everyone was settled, the server handed out menus and took their drink orders.

Russell asked for a bottle of pinot noir, and Irena, Paige, and Gail agreed to help him finish it. Brett and Jeffrey were fine with the water, and Alec decided that Scotch went with everything.

After reviewing the offerings, Alec decided on the crab and artichoke dip for an appetizer, the rack of lamb ambassador for his second course, and an apple torte for dessert. The others took longer to decide upon their meals.

While the diners were nibbling on rolls and waiting for their first course, Alec asked them how often their recipes were stolen.

Brett responded, "I've been fortunate, but my dad had to sue Bob Irwin. That man didn't even try to change my father's goat cheese tart recipe. He just copied and pasted it on his website word for word."

Jeffrey nodded. "It's not easy to win a lawsuit over a plagiarized recipe. Ingredients in most dishes don't vary much. People get into trouble when they copy directions that include personal references. Bob thought he could get away with it."

Gail interjected, "You were lucky to learn about it from Carlos."

"How much did Bob have to pay you?" Paige inquired.

"Not a lot," Jeffrey admitted. "Just an apology and a few thousand dollars. It irked me because it was for one of my wife's favorite recipes."

The dinner conversation changed when the appetizers arrived. Gail mentioned that her first job out of college was with Overeaters Anonymous. Brett asked many questions, and Alec learned the OA followed a twelve-step program like Gambler's Anonymous.

Unlike GA, Overeaters Anonymous was created to help people who have addictive behaviors towards food. It was not only for overeaters but also for those with anorexia and bulimia nervosa. Alec had no idea there were so many issues related to food consumption, and the compulsion to eat or not eat was often based on irrational beliefs.

Alec could understand why Brett had gravitated to comfort food after her mother died. Her food truck business expressed her wish to bring a sense of well-being to others.

Since food was needed to live, Alec asked Gail, "What foods should a person abstain from? A person can't just stop eating."

Gail named several trigger foods and events that encouraged people to overeat and explained, "The first step of the program is for its members to admit they have a problem."

Brett asked which diets OA recommended, and Gail answered, "The organization always advises members to speak to a doctor or dietician before going on a diet. In the past, I've recommended Weight Watchers and The South Beach diet. Even though OA wants people to accept that they can't do it alone, we'd remind them, 'We're powerless, not helpless.'"

In response, Brett teared up, and Jeffrey, visibly shaken by his daughter's emotional state, implored her to tell him what was troubling her. When Brett merely shrugged, Gail acknowledged, "It's hard to change your philosophy toward food.

"As a chef of comfort foods, you may want to consider making macaroni and cheese with whole-grain pasta and lower-fat cheese. With your creativity, you can make it even better than the original. You don't need to alter your belief that food should be comforting."

Brett, now smiling, rose to hug Gail and confessed, "I've been struggling with the desire to serve comforting meals that are *also* wholesome. I want to eat less fattening foods, too. I don't need to be skinny, but it would be wonderful to carry less weight around."

The waiter brought over their main course seconds later. Since Brett had ordered braised sole with leeks and saffron pilaf, she didn't need to curtail her appetite. The meals in the dining room were lovely-looking but also portion-controlled for diners who planned to eat all three courses. Passengers with eyes bigger than their stomachs often felt uncomfortably full upon leaving the dining room.

Over dessert, Irena asked the group, "What do you plan to do after dinner? Russell and I are going to attend the show in the Starlight Lounge. Singers and dancers will be doing a tribute to Canadian music artists. We want to see which songs have been included in the performance."

Russell added, "There's a chocolate extravaganza afterward in which treats of every description will be given out. I hope the old gal and I can stay up that late."

Irena tut-tutted her brother for his remark, "Old gal," and promised, "I plan to participate in all the activities. Tomorrow is a sea day, and I'm going to sleep in until the Pacific Northwest brunch is served at 10:00 AM!"

When Russell asked Brett and her dad whether they'd like to come, they agreed with a smile. As they rose to leave, Alec patted his stomach and said to Paige, "I think I ate too much again."

On the way to the Starlight Lounge, the ship's photographers asked them whether they wanted to have their pictures taken. Brett, who had been very careful with her appearance, stopped her father and said, "Let's take one together. I may never dress up like this again."

The two walked over to the cameraman and were told where to stand, put their hands, and place their heads. Though people often felt physically uncomfortable following those instructions, the photos usually came out well.

Afterward, Russell, Irena, and Paige posed for the camera. Gail didn't want to join them without Derek and Oliver and remarked, "We had our pictures taken on the first gala evening. We put Oliver in a little grey suit with a bowtie. He looked adorable and decided to grace us with a smile."

Paige demanded, "Make sure you have the ship make me a print." Russell seconded it.

The entourage proceeded to the lounge and saw it was filling up fast. Alec had to ask a couple to move over one seat to accommodate their party.

Paige filed in first, followed by Alec, Jeffrey, Brett, Russell, Irena, and Gail. Paige's sister-in-law wanted to be on the aisle, unsure she'd stay for the entire performance.

The house lights dimmed shortly later, and Faith Rossi appeared in front of the stage's closed curtains. The cruise director cautioned the audience from taking flash photos and remarked, "You're in for a real treat." With that said, she stepped off the stage, and the curtains opened.

Over the next seventy-five minutes, Alec and his guests heard musical selections that were originally sung by Celine Dion, Justin Bieber, Shania Twain, Bryan Adams, and Neil Young. Dancers made the songs more memorable by reimagining the famous lyrics.

Alec was especially moved when the entertainers performed Michael Bublé's hit, "Home." It didn't take Alec long to join the male artist and sing,

Another summer day
Has come and gone away
In Paris and Rome
But I wanna go home, mmm

May be surrounded by
A million people, I
Still feel all alone
Just wanna go home
Oh, I miss you, you know

And I've been keeping all the letters
That I wrote to you
Each one a line or two
I'm fine baby, how are you?

Well I would send them but I know
That it's just not enough
My words were cold and flat
And you deserve more than that

Another airplane
Another sunny place
I'm lucky I know
But I wanna go home
Mmm, I got to go home

Let me go home
I'm just too far
From where you are
I wanna come home

And I feel just like
I'm living someone else's life
It's like I just stepped outside
When everything was going right

And I know just why you could not

Come along with me
That this was not your dream
But you always believed in me

Another winter day
Has come and gone away
In even Paris and Rome
And I wanna go home
Let me go home

And I'm surrounded by
A million people I
I still feel alone
Oh, let me go home
Oh, I miss you, you know

Let me go home
I've had my run
Baby, I'm done
I gotta go home
Let me go home
It'll all be all right
I'll be home tonight
I'm coming back home

When the song ended, Alec noticed tears in Jeffrey's eyes. Surprised by his emotional display, Alec realized he was not as rigid and controlled as he pretended to be.

The final selection was much more upbeat, showcasing Joni Mitchell's "Big Yellow Taxi." At the end of the performance, Faith reappeared on stage to remind the audience to participate in the chocolate extravaganza at nine o'clock.

Alec and company headed to the Ocean Bar, which was midship, to await the goodies. Even though Gail was antsy to return to her baby and husband, she remained, deciding that Derek would be especially pleased to see her with a platter of sweets.

The chocolate extravaganza featured white, milk, and dark chocolate over nuts, pretzels, popcorn, and strawberries. Trays of fudge brownies, petit fours, and truffles were also displayed. The array was mind-boggling, and Irena had to stop sampling the treats, afraid that the chocolate's natural caffeine would keep her up at night.

Russell tried nearly everything, and Gail found a plate large enough to hold Derek's favorites. Alec and Paige just wanted a few brownies to enjoy later with decaf coffee. Brett, mindful of the calories, tasted just two as Jeffrey marveled at how the sweets were prepared and presented.

When the last few servers headed to the kitchen with empty trays, Alec and the others called it a night.

On returning to their suite, Paige removed her dressy clothes, and Alec started the coffee maker.

Wearing a robe, Paige joined Alec in their kitchen and asked, "Have you learned anything tonight that will help you name Irwin's killer?"

As Paige poured coffee into their mugs, Alec replied, "Right now, everything is jumbled up in my head. Let's review what was said over drinks and dinner."

Paige, taking a sip of the hot liquid, answered, "You found out that Jeffrey's wife, Peggy, had been a teacher at his culinary college, and he mixed pills and alcohol when he learned about her death. You also confirmed that Irwin got Brett into trouble over her fire safety certificate."

Alec took the opportunity to have one of the two brownies. Recalling what was discussed at dinner, Alec asked, "Did you know that Brett was upset about her weight?"

Paige nodded, "Gail told me. I didn't know she started to overeat when her mother passed away. I can understand how a teenager might gravitate to food. I'm thrilled Gail was able to help Brett reconcile her need to create comfort food with healthier options."

That leaves," Alec concluded, "Brett's remark about her dad's lawsuit. Although Bob Irwin had reason to dislike Jeffrey, I don't think either of the Webbers killed him."

Paige finished *her* brownie before Alec could take it and headed to the bathroom to run her bath. Alec remained in the kitchen to rinse out the dishes. As he was putting them away, the cabin phone rang.

With wet hands, Alec picked up the handset. Regina Hill's voice was at the other end. Sweetly, she said, " I got a response from our Human Resource Department. I tried you earlier. I hope this isn't a bad time."

Alec replied, "Not at all. Paige and I had dinner and went to the show. What did you find out?"

He listened for a few minutes and thanked his associate.

While still in the tub, Paige asked, "Who called?"

Full of information, Alec joined his wife and shared, "It was Regina. The HR records on Irwin were pretty much what we expected. The department had received many complaints about his behavior. Crew and passengers alike reported him for bullying. Among them was a charge made by Faith Rossi. Before Irwin could be fired from Flagship Cruise Line, he quit."

Alec continued, "Claude Bourdain was also in the ship's files. He was written up when Irwin accused him of purposely ruining some of his dishes. The matter was dropped when Irwin resigned."

Paige responded, "Do you think Bourdain has held a grudge all this time and decided to kill Bob after seeing him at his seven-course dinner?"

"That's hard to believe," Alec acknowledged. "Bourdain has worked hard to attain his current position, and he's not the kind of man to throw it away."

Getting nowhere fast, Alec suggested, "Let's relax and watch some news on TV."

As Paige rose to dry off, she warned, "The broadcast might make you even more glum."

CHAPTER FIFTEEN

"Carry On Wayward Son"
Words & Music by Kerry Livgren
Genre: Progressive Rock, Released: November 1976

Sunday Morning—10th of August
Alec and Paige awoke to the sound of their telephone alarm. As Paige silenced the ring, Alec asked, "It's nine-fifteen already?"

Sympathetically, Paige inquired, "What time did you fall asleep? I felt you toss and turn until the wee hours."

"I think it was about three. I'd better shower before your dad and aunt get here. Maybe the hot water will chase away the cobwebs in my head."

As Alec shuffled to the bathroom, Paige tidied up the bed and called after him. "I won't bother making coffee. You can get your fill at brunch."

The DunBartons were dressed and ready when Russell and Irena knocked on the door. Noting his son-in-law's expression, Russell asked Paige, "Is he worried about solving the murder?"

Paige nodded, and Russell, trying to be encouraging, said, "Don't worry, Son."

The words to the Kansas song came to Alec's mind, and he sang out,

Carry on my wayward son
There'll be peace when you are done
Lay your weary head to rest
Don't you cry no more

Once I rose above the noise and confusion
Just to get a glimpse beyond this illusion
I was soaring ever higher, but I flew too high

Though my eyes could see I still was a blind man
Though my mind could think I still was a mad man
I hear the voices when I'm dreaming
I can hear them say

Carry on my wayward son
There'll be peace when you are done
Lay your weary head to rest
Don't you cry no more

Masquerading as a man with a reason
My charade is the event of the season
And if I claim to be a wise man
Well, it surely means that I don't know

On a stormy sea of moving emotion
Tossed about, I'm like a ship on the ocean
I set a course for winds of fortune
But I hear the voices say

Carry on my wayward son
There'll be peace when you are done
Lay your weary head to rest
Don't you cry no more no!

Carry on
You will always remember
Carry on
Nothing equals the splendor
Now your life's no longer empty

Surely heaven waits for you

Carry on my wayward son
There'll be peace when you are done
Lay your weary head to rest
Don't you cry
Don't you cry no more

Though Alec hadn't given up on finding Irwin's killer, he was mindful that time was running out. Aunt Irena got him out of his funk when she suggested, "You'll feel better when you have something to eat."

The foursome had to wait in line at the maître d's kiosk to have the dining room's special Pacific Northwest brunch. Since the restaurant was near capacity, Russell agreed to share a table of six with two other passengers.

Alec and his tablemates were looking over the menu when a server escorted two women to the table. Alec was thrilled that the newcomers were Bella Valentino and Nancy Lawton.

They seemed just as pleased to be with Alec and his family. Everyone had something to say about the brunch's offerings. There were toasted sandwiches, pancakes, crabcakes, and egg dishes with reindeer sausage and Alaskan salmon.

Alec decided upon the blueberry pancakes, confident they would be less sweet than a stack of banana fosters. He was glad to see that his tablemates had chosen more exotic dishes. This way, Alec could taste them with his eyes.

While the waiters filled their cups with hot coffee and took tea orders, Alec asked Bella about the time she was stalked and commented, "It must have been awful for you."

Glad she didn't ask who told him, Bella agreed. "It was terrifying. I don't mind having fans, but the fellow went much too far. At first, I thought it could have been Bob."

"Bob, Robert Irwin? " Alec stammered.

Bella replied, "Yes, him. It happened a few weeks after Bob moved to California. I've never trusted him and wondered whether he had hoped to win me back after our short affair in London. I was pretty relieved when I learned it was a different man."

Nancy added, "I remember how shaken Bella was from the episode. It was even worse when Bob became a member a year later. He was so full of himself, and Bella was *not* happy about it!"

Bella took a moment to pat Nancy's hand in affection and said, "I can't say I'm sorry he's dead. None of our members miss him."

When Nancy's Monte Cristo sandwich arrived, she confessed, "Whenever I was alone with Irwin, I felt like a long-tailed cat in a room of rocking chairs. You never knew how he was going to act or behave."

Irena grinned, "That's a wonderful way to describe it."

The tablemates became quiet while they dug into their meals. Alec was disappointed that just a few Alaskan blueberries adorned his pancakes. After sampling Paige's crab and hot smoked salmon cakes, he pronounced them delicious.

Over dessert, Bella said to the others, "Don't forget to come to our cooking competition in the Culinary Arts Center at two this afternoon. Our group will be competing against members of the San Francisco chapter. It's a three-part contest in which Carlos will prepare an appetizer; Nancy, a dessert; and me, the main entrée."

Just as enthusiastic as Bella, Nancy claimed, "I don't know how we can lose. Chef Bourdain is going to give us a basket of Alaskan ingredients that must be used in each dish. The concept is based on Food Network's, "Chopped.""

Irena gushed, "I love that program. Russell and I wouldn't miss it for the world."

Alec also promised that he and Paige would attend the cookoff and asked, "Who's judging it, and what will the winning team get?"

Shyly, Bella explained, "Claude can't judge us since we're dating. Two of his assistants and the pastry chef have offered to act as judges. The winning team is going to receive some of the ship's cookbooks. We want to win for the bragging rights!"

At 11:15 AM, the diners went their separate ways. Bella and Nancy had a meeting in the Hudson Room to discuss their strategies for the upcoming competition. Paige, Irena, and Russell announced their plans to go to the Starlight Lounge at 11:30 to hear a presentation on their final destination: Victoria, Canada.

Eager to learn about "The Garden City," Paige asked Alec whether he could join them. Feeling he should be doing something to find Irwin's killer, Alec turned her down and said he'd be in his office. As he was departing,. Paige called after him, "Don't be late for the culinary competition. We'll save you a seat."

Regina noticed Alec's downtrodden expression when he entered the room and guessed, "You're stuck, aren't you?"

Alec nodded, and Regina asked, "What can I do to help?"

"Perhaps," Alec suggested, 'I should write down what each of my suspects had against Robert Irwin. I think his death was premeditated. His killer must have come on board the ship with a vial of potassium chloride and a hypodermic needle. Therefore, it's unlikely that Faith Rossi or Claude Bourdain did it."

Regina disagreed. "It would shorten your number of suspects, but Bella could have told Claude that Robert Irwin booked this cruise. Faith could have noticed his name on this trip's manifest."

Alec acknowledged she was right and said, "All my suspects had an opportunity to kill Irwin. Zuma checked where they were between 11:00 PM and 1:00 AM on the night of Bob's death. According to their keycards, they were out and about for some of that time. It would have taken just seconds to inject KCL into Irwin's neck.

Regina smiled, "I leave you to it. When you finish, let me see what you've written."

Thankfully, Alec opened the Word program on his computer and began:

Irwin's Past and Suspects' Possible Motives

Robert Irwin
Disliked by everyone in his SV chapter
Suspected of being a stalker in California

Arrested and jailed for drunk driving in New York
Cited and given community service for ABH in London
Arrested and fined in London for selling anabolic steroids
Forced to leave FCL's Aquarius before HR could fire him
Abused anabolic steroids (injectables and pills)

Bella Valentino
Motive: To get rid of Irwin's uncomfortable presence
Could have reported Irwin over the warning label on power meals
May have known about Claude's prior relationship with Irwin
Thought Robert Irwin was capable of stalking her in CA
Had a destructive love affair with Irwin in London
Might have blamed Irwin for her husband's death

Jeffrey Webber
Motive: To punish Irwin for disrespecting him and Brett
Could have reported Irwin over the warning label on power meals
Sued and forced Irwin to pay $2,000 for plagiarizing his recipe
Angry that Irwin had tried to hurt his daughter's business

Brett Webber
Motive: To punish Irwin for disrespecting her and father
Could have reported Irwin over the warning label on power meals
Aware Irwin stole her father's recipe and was sued
Knew Irwin held up the opening of her food truck
business over inspection certificate

Carlos Ruiz
Motive: To inherit Irwin's portion of the business valued over 200K
Could have reported Irwin over the warning label on power meals
Was forced to pay cross-purchase insurance on Irwin's life
Annoyed that his meals did not legally belong to him
Upset that Irwin refused to let him out of his contract

Mei Chung
Motive: To end Irwin's blackmail and risk of being arrested
Promised to pay him after returning to California
Was being blackmailed by Irwin over her insider trading
Worried about losing her job & connection to her employer's sons
Could have reported Irwin over the warning label on power meals

Nancy Lawton
Motive: To prevent Irwin from ruining her life and Mei's
Agreed that Mei should pay blackmail over insider trading
Culpable for putting the stock sale under her name
Could have reported Irwin over the warning label on power meals

Claude Bourdain
Motive: To avenge past and possibly new grievances
May have been aware of Irwin's past relationship with Bella
Had angry words with Irwin at the "Dinner with the Exec. Chef"
Knew that Irwin tried to get him fired while on the Aquarius
Might have blamed Irwin for his breakup with Faith
Was upset that Faith had sex with Irwin

Faith Rossi
Motive: To avenge Irwin for physically overpowering her
Felt Irwin's actions contributed to her breakup with Claude
Was sexually assaulted by Irwin on the Aquarius

When Alec finished the Word document, he printed it and murmured, "I may have left out a few things."

Eagerly, Regina took the sheet of paper from Alec's outstretched hand. After glimpsing at it, she surmised, "Some of the motives sound pretty weak. Faith may have had the strongest one. Irwin took advantage of her when she was drunk. It could be the reason she never married. Sexual assault, even if she didn't say no, can stay with you a lifetime."

Alec pointed out, "Bella may have blamed herself for getting involved with Irwin so soon after her husband's death. I know from experience that it's easy to make poor decisions after losing a loved one."

Regina nodded and then asked, "Do you think Irwin could have caused the death of Bella's husband?"

"It's one of the things bothering me," Alec replied. "Bella's husband, Tony Valentino, went to the same health club as Irwin, and the two had been friends. I keep wondering whether the bodybuilder encouraged him to take one of his drugs or participate in a strenuous exercise. Tony died from a ruptured brain aneurysm. I read that heavy lifting or straining can cause a weak artery to burst."

Alec added, "It's speculation, but Bella may suspect the same thing."

Regina offered, "It's certainly possible. Mei Chung and Nancy Lawton also had a good reason to want Bob Irwin dead. He could have bled them dry over their insider trading."

Alec found his conversation with Regina very helpful and asked whether she felt the Webbers could have been responsible. Regina replied, "Not with what you wrote. Disrespect is not a motive for murder. Have you found out how and when Jeffrey's wife died?"

"Not yet," Alec acknowledged, "In Nicola's email, she wrote that Robert Irwin was arrested in NY for seriously injuring a woman named Margaret Downey. He was intoxicated at the time, pled guilty, and was jailed for a short time. I'll try to have a word with Brett this afternoon and find out how her mom died."

Realizing that the ACA competition was scheduled to begin soon, Alec recapped, "That just leaves Ruiz. If money were the motive, he would win hands down. According to their business contract, Irwin was insured for over two hundred thousand dollars—a tidy sum by anyone's reckoning."

As Alec was heading out the door, "Regina called. "I know you're getting close to finding Bob's killer. Don't give up!"

CHAPTER SIXTEEN

▼

"No Time"

Words & Music by Randy Bachman and Burton Cummings
Genre: Pop Rock, Released: September 1969

Sunday Afternoon—10th of August

Alec arrived at the Culinary Arts Center at 1:45 PM. Quite a few people were milling around the semicircle lounge. In front of the stage were two complete mini kitchens. Each had four electric burners, a fry station, a large sink, and a four-foot workspace.

To the left of the burners were an oven/broiler and microwave, stacked on each other. Video cameras were positioned above and in front of the galley to catch the competitor's actions.

In between the kitchens was a stainless-steel rack loaded with foodstuffs. Alec noticed Paige and her family gazing at the items in the pantry and joined them. A list of ingredients was beside the rack. Alec's eyes glossed over it and read,

Pantry Goods:
Dairy:
    Butter
    Cheese (several varieties)

    Cream Cheese
    Eggs
    Half and Half
    Heavy Cream
    Mascarpone
    Mayonnaise
    Milk
    Sour Cream
    Yogurt
Fresh Fruits:
    Apples
    Bananas
    Berries (several varieties)
    Citrus (several varieties)
    Pears
    Stone fruit (several varieties)
Fresh Vegetables:
    Broccoli
    Brussels Sprouts
    Carrots
    Cauliflower
    Celery
    Garlic
    Ginger
    Green Beans
    Herbs (several varieties)
    Leafy Greens (several varieties)
    Mushrooms (several varieties
    Onions
    Parsley
    Peppers (several varieties)
    Scallions
    Tomatoes
    Yams
Protein Rich Sources:
    Beef (several cuts)
    Fish
    Lamb
    Poultry
    Seafood (several varieties)
    Smoked Meats

Staples:
    Baking Powder/Soda
    Bread (several varieties)
    Bread Crumbs
    Canned Beans (several varieties)
    Canned Olives
    Capers
    Chocolate/Cocoa
    Coffee
    Cornstarch
    Dried Fruit (several varieties)
    Flour
    Honey
    Mustard
    Noodles
    Nuts (several varieties)
    Oatmeal
    Oils (several varieties)
    Pancake Mix
    Pastas (several varieties)
    Rice
    Salt/Pepper
    Sauces (several varieties)
    Seltzer
    Soy Sauce
    Spices (several varieties)
    Stock
    Sugar
    Tea
    Vinegar (several varieties)
    Wine (red and white)

Alec was amazed at how many products had been gathered from the kitchen and brought to the Culinary Arts Center. Alec, familiar with the TV show, "Chopped," knew that the contestants could enhance their basket ingredient dishes with additional food items.

Faith Rossi appeared in the lounge at two o'clock sharp and had the audience members take their seats. Paige directed Alec to a row of four chairs that had personal belongings on each. While Irena and Russell promptly sat, Paige patted the chair beside her and said, "This one is for you."

Alec smiled as he lifted off her sweater and replied, "Do you want to wear it? It's chilly in here."

Paige placed it over her shoulders and waited in rapt attention for the cruise director to say more.

On cue, Faith announced, "Welcome to the American Catering Association culinary contest. On this cruise, two local chapters of the ACA are sailing with us. One group is from San Francisco, California, and the others are from neighboring Silicon Valley.

"Today, the caterers will be given basket ingredients like the chefs on Food Network's television show, "Chopped." Instead of having one chef make an appetizer, entrée, and dessert, the teams have appointed three members to prepare a dish in each category."

She paused for effect and said, "Let's give our contestants a big hand."

From behind one side of the stage's curtains, three caterers emerged. Faith pointed to two men and one woman and declared, "This group of chefs are members of the San Francisco chapter. Lydia will be making an appetizer, Paul, the entrée, and Jordan, dessert."

Alec had seen them before at the ACA joint activities but knew little about them. Paul was the chapter's president, and Alec found himself looking forward to his competition with Bella.

Next, Faith announced the names of those competing from Silicon Valley and called Carlos, Bella, and Nancy, in turn. They stepped forward to the sound of applause.

When it died down, Faith resumed. "The contestants will now be given ten minutes to become familiar with the foodstuffs and their location on the steel rack. Feel free to talk amongst yourselves for this part of the presentation."

Alec had his eyes peeled on the six caterers as they handled some of the produce and checked out the fresh herbs. The time flew by, and it seemed like only seconds before Faith declared,

"Our Senior Executive Chef, Claude Bourdain, has amassed some unusual Northwest Pacific ingredients for each basket."

The appetizer contestants were then instructed to go to their kitchens. Faith had the remaining four take seats to the right of the audience. Since there were no basket hampers in the kitchens, Alec waited for someone to bring them out.

Faith brought the audience's attention to the back of the lounge and revealed the names and titles of the three judges who entered the room. The judge, carrying appetizer baskets, deposited one on each workstation. He then sat with the other two men at a table to the left of the stage.

It was 2:15 PM when Faith informed Lydia and Carlos to open their baskets. As they removed the ingredients, Faith announced, "They've been given steamed Dungeness crab, sea chickweed, rutabaga, and Skiff Light Lager from Harbor Mountain Brewery in Sitka, Alaska."

Like most professional chefs, Lydia and Carlos tasted the lager and sea chickweed before rushing to the pantry to get additional ingredients for a dish that was forming in their minds. Alec's eyes went from one video screen to the other, similar to a spectator watching a tennis match.

Alec heard gasps from Irena as the caterers chopped vegetables with ultra-sharp knives and ran to the pantry for missing items. The appetizer competitors had only twenty minutes to prepare and plate.

Gazing at his watch, Alec murmured to Paige, "Do you think Carlos will finish in time? He still has something in his fryer."

Hurriedly, Ruiz removed the blistering hot food with his bare hands and placed it on a bed of salad. "Paige squealed, "He must have hands of asbestos."

Alec agreed. When the time was called, Faith approached Carlos and asked what he prepared. He lifted one of the plates under the video camera so everyone could see his dish.

With self-assurance, Carlos pronounced, "I diced the rutabaga, pickled it, and added it to the crab mixture of mascarpone cheese and seasoning. The mixture was formed into small balls and fried in beer batter. They're sitting on a bed of sea chickweed that was sautéed in oil with onions and garlic."

The audience clapped loudly, and Alec turned to see ACA members from both groups standing at the back of the lounge. The dishes were brought to the judge's table. After tasting them, they filled in a form that rated up to ten points for plating and twenty for gameplay and taste.

Lydia, appearing nervous, told the judges she had braised a tomato in lager and filled it with a mixture of crabmeat and pasta. On top of the tomato were deep-fried pieces of sea chickweed and, to its side, pickled rutabaga salad.

Alec thought both dishes were imaginative and realized he'd have to wait until the end of the contest to find out how each caterer did. Before the second group of competitors could be called, staff from the dining room cleaned the mini kitchens and brought out the next basket containing Alaskan and Canadian ingredients.

Shortly later, Bella and Paul were allowed to go to their cooking areas and open the entrée basket. Faith called out, "The chefs have been given raw salmon fillets, reindeer milk cheese, fresh rhubarb, and kasha or buckwheat groats, which was brought over to Sitka by Russian settlers in the 1800s."

The caterers rushed over to the pantry items, collected what they wanted, and returned to their workstations with full arms. Bella had gathered white wine, vinegar, soy sauce, and honey. Alec turned to Paige to whisper, "I think she's going in an Asian direction. It won't be easy for her to incorporate the cheese."

Paige replied, "I wonder what Paul will do."

They soon learned from Faith that Paul planned to make salmon fillets with a green sauce composed of reindeer cheese, herbs, and capers. It remained to be seen how he hoped to incorporate the rhubarb and kasha.

The chefs were given thirty minutes to prepare their dishes. Despite the extra time, they were breathless when the cruise director counted down the seconds. Paul was asked to present his dish to the judges and brought over salmon encrusted in kasha. The green sauce was drizzled over the salmon and served with a tangy rhubarb salad. The judges had satisfied smiles as they jotted down Paul's score.

Bella followed. Although Alec had gotten used to Bella's scanty outfits, he wondered whether the judges were professional enough to ignore her cleavage as she bent down to serve them. She had created a caramelized teriyaki salmon dish with sesame-toasted kasha. A roasted rhubarb and reindeer cheese salad accompanied it.

Alec watched the judges with rapt attention and couldn't decide from their expressions whether they liked her meal. While the kitchens were tidied up again and the dessert baskets placed on each counter, the audience members took the opportunity to speak to each other.

Irena was particularly interested in seeing what Nancy planned to whip up, and Russell declared, "That Bella is something else!"

Unsure what his father-in-law meant, Alec asked and learned that Russell, a widower of many years, still found Bella highly desirable. Realizing he was not immune to a woman's charms, Alec chuckled.

The third and final round began when Faith announced that Nancy and a young man named Jordan were called up. When they opened their baskets, Faith revealed. "The chefs have been given wild Alaskan blueberries, Canadian maple syrup, Aurora gin, and previously baked bear claw pastries."

Jordan was faster than Nancy in grabbing the items he needed for his dessert. She appeared more thoughtful despite having just twenty minutes to create her masterpiece. Nancy tasted the gin and added it to a saucepan containing maple syrup and blueberries. The bear claws, filled with marzipan, were cut into slices, dipped into a cinnamon egg mixture, and fried in butter.

The male chef took a different tact and soaked diced cubes of bear claws in gin and maple syrup. It didn't take Alec long to pronounce to Paige, "He's making a trifle. How clever."

Paige nodded as she watched Jordan make lemon custard and whipped cream. He macerated the blueberries, tasted them, and added maple syrup to sweeten them. The audience oohed and aahed as he layered his concoctions in clear glass bowls.

Nancy seemed put out by the onlooker's reaction and stepped up her game by candying pecans. She placed the French toasted bear claws on a plate, spooned blueberry compote over it, and topped it with candied pecans, fresh blueberries, and whipped cream.

Alec's mouth watered as the judges tasted the completed desserts and finished scoring. The appetizer contestants were called up to the judge's table first and told their scores. Carlos received a total of 46 and Lydia 43. Carlos could not disguise his jubilation, and Alec momentarily felt sorry for the woman.

On the main entrée, Paul edged Bella out by one point, 44 to 43. Jordan's trifle scored 45, and Nancy's French toast and blueberry dessert a 42. Nancy appeared annoyed over the ranking and gave the judges a look that could kill. Alec was astonished to see her vehement reaction and asked himself, "Could she have killed Robert Irwin over a small slight?"

The primary judge tallied the grand score and announced, "We had a very close competition and enjoyed all the dishes. The creativity of our contestants was awe-inspiring. For those of you who are math impaired, the cookoff winner was the San Francisco chapter of the ACA with 132 points. The Silicon Valley caters received 131 points."

As the audience applauded, Bella shook hands with the winning team. Despite losing, Carlos seemed thrilled about receiving the highest score among the caterers.

The ACA members in the back of the lounge joined their comrades while Faith announced, "Thank you for coming to this culinary event. Please enjoy the rest of your day at sea. Tomorrow, we'll be in Victoria, British Columbia, and return to Seattle on Tuesday."

As Alec and his entourage exited the Culinary Arts Center, he noticed Mei Chung with Nancy Lawton. Neither woman looked happy.

Outside the room, Alec and his family made a beeline to the Starlight Lounge to attend a discussion on Victorian. It was going to be the DunBarton's last day of vacation before returning to the crew of the Pegasus, and Alec wanted to make the most of it. They decided to join Irena and Russell on a city tour, including afternoon tea at the famous Empress Hotel.

With those plans made, Aunt Irena and Russell rushed off to babysit Oliver so his parents could attend the ACA dinner at the ship's Bulldog Pub. Left alone, Alec and Paige decided to have an early dinner at the Lido buffet.

At the informal eatery, Alec just picked at his meal. Having seen the signs before, Paige remarked, "I know you're stumped and are worrying you won't find Irwin's killer in time."

Alec looked miserable as he sang,

(No time left for you)
On my way to better things
(No time left for you)
I'll find myself some wings
(No time left for you)
Distant roads are calling me
(No time left for you)

No time for a summer friend
No time for the love you send
Seasons change and so did I
You need not wonder why
You need not wonder why
There's no time left for you
No time left for you

(No time left for you)
On my way to better things
(No time left for you)
I'll find myself some wings
(No time left for you)
Distant roads are calling me
(No time left for you)

No time for a gentle rain
No time for my watch and chain
No time for revolving doors
No time for the killing floor
No time for the killing floor
There's no time left for you
No time left for you

No time for a summer friend
No time for the love you send
Seasons change and so did I
You need not wonder why
You need not wonder why
There's no time left for you
No time left for you

Paige smiled weakly and encouraged, "Eat up. Afterward, I'll buy you a drink at the Lido Bar. You can smoke there and try out the blueberry-flavored pipe tobacco I bought you in Alaska."

Alec smiled at the thought and dug into his dinner.

Once seated on the cushioned lounge chairs, the DunBartons summoned the server and ordered their usuals. Alec was in the midst of stuffing his briar pipe when the drinks arrived.

Even though the air was slightly chilly, the sun was intense. Paige stretched like a contented kitten in her raglan-sleeve sweater while Alec took a large sip of his Glenlivet.

Like a pro, Alec lit his pipe with one match, partially inhaled, and exhaled a near-perfect smoke circle. They were brought out of their reverie when Alec's cell phone rang.

Alec answered, "DunBarton here," and was startled to hear Nicola Campbell's voice on the line. Paige gazed at him as he responded with words like "not yet," "really," and "no."

When Alec signaled Paige for a pen and paper, she dove into her tote bag. After finding what he needed, she was instructed to write down, "Alaska Air, Juneau to Seattle, Flight AA 66, and Arrival 10:21 PM."

Alec listened to the deputy chief a few minutes more and then replied, "It's good you're coming tomorrow night. I'll meet you and your associate from the Seattle Homicide Department at the ship's crew entrance at 7:30 AM on Tuesday."

When the call ended, Paige, full of questions, asked, "Does she know you haven't solved the murder yet?"

Alec nodded but added, "Nicola learned that Margaret Downey, the woman driven off the road in New York by Robert Irwin, was Webber's wife, Peggy. Downey was her maiden name, and it hadn't occurred to me that Peggy was a nickname for Margaret. That poor woman experienced severe head trauma from the car accident and ended up in a persistent vegetative state. Unlike a coma, PVS sufferers appear to be conscious but have no cognitive function."

Paige shivered, "It must have been awful for Brett and her dad to see Peggy in that condition. What happened to her?"

Alec, taking another mouthful of his drink, answered, "She died ten months later from organ failure." Relighting his pipe, he added, "If Jeffrey knew that Irwin caused his wife's death, he's moving to the top of my suspect list!"

CHAPTER SEVENTEEN

▼

"Helplessly Hoping"
Words & Music by Stephen Stills
Genre: Folk Rock, Released: June 1969

__Monday Morning—11th of August__

Alec was unable to track down Jeffrey Webber until the morning. By the time he located him in the dining room, Alec was in an awful mood. The caterer was sitting alone, finishing his coffee.

Though Alec was hungry himself, he took an empty chair and demanded, "Why didn't you tell me that Irwin caused your wife's death?"

Webber remained calm despite Alec's attitude and replied, "I didn't see the need. I confronted him years ago, and he was punished. It was an accident, and Peggy would have been the first to forgive him. She was an incredibly loving woman."

Alec couldn't believe what he was hearing. Jeffrey must have been angry when his wife was hospitalized and later died.

Still indignant, Alec asked, "What happened when he joined your chapter of the ACA? Were you surprised to see him?"

With more animation, Jeffrey agreed, "I was startled. At first, he didn't recognize me. When I reminded him how we originally met, he showed consternation and apologized. I can't say I was pleased to see him again. I tried to keep out of his way, and he mine."

"What about your daughter?" Alec probed. "How much did you tell her?"

Ignoring Alec's question, Webber rose from his chair and walked away. Alec caught up with him in the dining room's foyer and insisted, "Did she know?"

Now red in the face, Jeffrey turned to Alec and warned, "Keep away from her! She had nothing to do with Irwin's death. Talk to Bella. She saw your cruise director milling around the spa when Bob died."

It was 10:00 AM when Alec ferreted out Bella Valentino on the Lido Deck. She was at a table beside the pool with Nancy Lawton. Alec told them to remain where they were while he hurried to the buffet to pick up eggs, bacon, and hash browns.

They were still at the table when Alec joined them. Full of curiosity, Bella asked, "What's gotten you so excited?"

Alec took a moment to sample his breakfast and replied, "I just spoke to Jeffrey. He told me that you saw Faith Rossi near the fitness center when Irwin was murdered. Is that true? Why didn't you tell me?"

Bella smiled halfheartedly. "I didn't want you to think I had anything to do with Robert's death. I decided to give Bob a piece of my mind after he was so rude to Claude at our seven-course dinner. I was about to take the hallway to the gym when I spotted the cruise director."

"What time was that?" Alec delved.

Bella shook her head and offered, "Maybe eleven-thirty? The spa was closed, and on spotting Faith, I decided to speak to Bob in the morning. I returned to my cabin shortly afterward."

"How was Faith behaving when you noticed her?"

"Okay," Bella replied. "She had her back to me when I passed through the spa's foyer. I saw her face reflected in the glass case containing beauty products." Now asking a question of her own, she posed, "Did she murder Robert?"

Feeling he was finally getting somewhere, Alec inquired, "Did Claude tell you much about his past relationship with Faith?"

Nancy, quiet up to then, said, "Do you want me to leave?"

Bella patted her hand and replied, "It's not necessary. I'll only have to fill you in later."

The women smiled at each other, and Alec listened to Bella as she revealed, "Claude told me that he and Faith were once engaged. She never married and recently broke up with Security Chief Zuma when he wanted to get more serious. He thinks Faith may have some form of PTSD—post-traumatic stress disorder."

Alec found her remarks telling and thanked Bella for her candor. It left Alec in a quandary. Did Faith cover up the one camera in the gym that would have given away her presence? As a crew member, she would have been aware of it. Alec couldn't be sure of Zuma either. Did he know more about Irwin's murder than he was saying? How could he investigate Faith and keep the security officer out of the loop?

Since the captain wanted an update, Alec decided to speak to him next. After scheduling to see him at noon, Alec set off for the infirmary to find Dr. Abbot.

The doctor was in and immediately invited Alec into his inner sanctum after telling the nurse on duty, "Don't disturb me unless it's urgent."

When his office door closed behind him, Douglas queried, "Do you know who killed Robert Irwin?"

As they took seats, Alec replied, "I think it was Faith Rossi."

"Our Faith," the doctor gaped. "Why would she do such a thing?"

Alec spent the next few minutes telling Douglas that Faith may have changed her outlook on life after having an unwanted sexual encounter with Irwin. Though it had happened years ago, Alec asked the medic about PTSD and how it manifested itself."

Still unsettled that Faith could be a killer, Douglas explained, "People living with PTSD often have intrusive memories of the past, avoid painful activities, feel numb or have negative thoughts about themselves, and/or undergo physical symptoms such as sweating, rapid breathing, and fast heartbeats.

"It doesn't only happen to soldiers who have returned from war. It can be seen in people who are stressed or come across reminders of a past traumatic event."

Alec nodded. "If Faith saw Irwin's name on a passenger list, could she have felt driven to do something drastic?" Awkwardly, Alec added, "I know you can't talk about a patient's care, but is it possible she was clinically depressed?"

Douglas frowned. Although Alec didn't get a response, the doctor's body language led him to believe that Faith was being treated for something. This was partially confirmed when Dr. Abbot shared, "Harold encouraged her to see a therapist after their breakup."

Getting to the subject at hand, Alec asked Douglas, "Do you think I should let Zuma know that I suspect Faith? I don't have proof she murdered Irwin, but she had motive and opportunity."

Under his breath, Alec added, "I plan to ask Deputy Campbell to get a warrant to search her cabin. She and a Seattle homicide officer are going to board the Pegasus tomorrow morning."

Douglas replied, "You've answered your own question. Advise the captain and let the Juneau policewomen do the dirty work. Stewart and Zuma will not be happy if Faith is a killer. I don't envy you!"

Alec was a few minutes early when he stepped into the captain's ready room. Puzzled, Stewart asked, "Where's Chief of Security Zuma? Isn't he coming?"

Wearing a grave expression, Alec revealed, "I haven't invited him to join us."

The captain must have noticed Alec's demeanor and had him take a seat at his meeting room table before probing, "Is he involved in the murder?"

Quickly, Alec replied, "I don't think so, but I'm coming to believe that Faith Rossi is guilty."

The captain joined Alec at the table and murmured, "I see. What proof do you have?"

Alec brought Stewart up to date about Rossi's past issues with Robert Irwin and the recent events that could have worsened her PTSD. Instead of being annoyed that the ship's reputation may suffer, the captain expressed sorrow.

Seeing that as a good sign, Alec related Campbell's plan to board the ship in Seattle. He agreed with their course of action and warned Alec to keep him advised.

On leaving the Navigation Deck, Alec sang out,

Helplessly hoping
Her harlequin hovers nearby
Awaiting a word
Gasping at glimpses
Of gentle true spirit
He runs, wishing he could fly
Only to trip at the sound of good-bye

Wordlessly watching
He waits by the window
And wonders
At the empty place inside
Heartlessly helping himself to her bad dreams
He worries
Did he hear a good-bye? Or even hello?

They are one person
They are two alone
They are three together
They are for each other

Stand by the stairway
You'll see something
Certain to tell you confusion has its cost
Love isn't lying
It's loose in a lady who lingers
Saying she is lost

And choking on hello

They are one person
They are two alone
They are three together
They are for each other

Despite being concerned about Faith's prospects, Alec decided to enjoy his last vacation day. After contacting Nicola Campbell on the phone and updating her on the latest events, he returned to his cabin to prepare for his Grand City Drive & Empress Hotel High Tea Excursion in Victoria.

Paige greeted her husband and wanted to know how he made out with Jeffrey Webber. On hearing that Faith Rossi may have been responsible for Irwin's death, Paige shared Alec's sadness.

"Still," she encouraged, "let's get ready for our outing. I don't want to disappoint my father and Aunt Irena. We're supposed to meet them on the pier at 1:30 PM, and the tea is at three. Have you had any lunch? I don't want you to overeat and spoil your appetite for later."

Alec agreed but replied, "The eggs I had at breakfast aren't going to hold me long. Do you have anything I can nosh on now?"

As Paige was packing her tote bag, she directed Alec to the fridge, where there was a leftover Cuban sandwich, and asked, "Will that do? There are also some cookies and chips in the pantry."

Alec was more than happy with his meal and finished it by the time Paige called from the door, "Time's a-wastin.'"

Upon disembarking the ship, Alec and Paige were welcomed to Victoria by a large sign. After walking through a building containing souvenirs, they came across a parking lot congested with tour buses.

Paige was glad to see her aunt and father already there, thumbing through Canadian vacation guides and pamphlets. The air was misty, and the temperature uncomfortably cool. They really couldn't complain after having above-normal weather in Alaska.

Putting on her hooded windbreaker, Paige asked her aunt whether she wanted the umbrella she had stuffed in her tote bag. Irena smiled, "I like this weather. It reminds me of Maine."

Irena added, "I can't believe I'm flying home tomorrow. I loved being with you and the family."

Alec understood her feelings and asked, "Are you sure you don't want to stay longer?"

Russell agreed, "You can stay with me as long as you like."

Irena paused a moment before replying, "No. I think I'm ready to go back to Boothbay Harbor. Summer is short there, and I miss my friends." Sentimentally, she added, "It would be nice to come back at Christmas and see how much Oliver has grown."

Russell promised, "That's a date. When we reboard the ship, we're going to book it. It's much easier to leave when you have plans to return."

Alec was happy to see it settled and even happier when Bella and Claude Bourdain walked over to them. They, too, had tickets to go on the city tour and afternoon tea. Having questions for the executive chef, Alec whispered, "I'd like to chat with you later about your relationship with Robert Irwin and Faith Rossi."

Claude nodded and said, "Bella told me she saw Faith near the gym when Irwin died and shared it with you. I may be able to fill in some gaps."

Their conversation was cut short when an English double-decker bus pulled up. A woman in her sixties descended the vehicle's steps and welcomed the group of twenty. After checking the tickets, she invited the passengers to take seats wherever they wished.

Irena and Russell opted to stay on the lower level, and the DunBartons followed the others to the upper deck via a metallic circular staircase. Paige voiced, "I hope my dad and aunt don't mind. You get a better view of the city from here."

As the bus took off, the tour guide revealed, "My name is Cora. I've lived on Vancouver Island most of my life. I was raised nearby and, when I married, returned to my place of birth. Although Victoria has changed over the years, it has remained one of the best small cities in which to reside. Victoria is known as the City of Gardens."

From Alec's viewpoint, he could see tall poles holding large baskets of flowers. The colors were astounding, and Alec wondered how many city workers were needed to tend them. Since Cora was on the lower level, that question remained unasked.

While going through Beacon Hill Park, she explained, "The park is 740,000 square meters of green space and activities. It's meticulously landscaped and full of family-friendly attractions, including gardens, walking trails, playgrounds, a petting zoo, and a water park. The local wildlife includes blue herons, swans, turtles, deer, and peacocks."

From the park, the passengers were taken to the downtown area. They saw the Inner Harbor, a wide pedestrian street, the Royal British Columbia Museum, the BC Parliament Building, and Chinatown.

Cora stated that Victoria's Chinatown was the oldest in Canada and pointed out Fan Tan Alley. The street was not only infamous for its gambling and opium dens but also its size—three feet wide and the narrowest commercial street in North America.

Their final stop was the luxurious and historic Empress Hotel, built in 1908. The sightseers were excited about entering the architectural gem. It had begun to rain, and the tearoom was inviting, with its tall white columns, fabric-upholstered seating, and large windows.

The tables accommodated two to six individuals, and delicate bone China teacups and plates were set up on them. Russell and Irena were the first to ask for a large table and induced Alec, Paige, Bella, and Claude to join them. Irena winked at Alec, guessing he wanted to speak to the executive chef.

The servers descended on them with pots of English tea and three-tiered cake stands full of small savory sandwiches, freshly baked scones, and signature pastries. Initially, no one talked as they looked over the offerings.

After tasting a few, everyone had something to say about their mushroom quiche, smoked salmon blini, and pistachio opera cake. When the ladies and Russell announced their desire to look around the hotel, Alec used the time to have his tête-à-tête with Claude.

The executive chef was forthcoming and clarified, "You might have been misled by some of Faith's remarks about me. I want to explain that I didn't break up with her when Robert assaulted her. I didn't hold her responsible.

"I broke our engagement five months later. Faith had learned she was pregnant, and I had begged her to keep the baby. I didn't care whether Bob or I had impregnated her and promised to bring up the child as my own.

"Originally, Faith seemed okay with it. She changed her mind midway through the pregnancy and got an abortion in London without consulting me. I couldn't marry her knowing she had lied to me and took the life of an innocent."

Alec nodded as Claude continued, "Faith had health issues afterward and found out she had a condition known as Asherman's Syndrome. It's when internal scarring makes it impossible for a woman to have children. Even though she was partly responsible, Faith placed most of the blame on Irwin."

From Claude's remarks, Alec decided that Faith had a strong motive to want Irwin dead and asked, "Did you know she's currently dealing with depression?"

Claude conceded, "I might have made things worse. A few months ago, I told her I met a lovely woman, and she planned to sail with us in August. I didn't want Faith to hear of it through our grapevine."

On checking his watch, Alec realized the bus was scheduled to pick them up in minutes. Before joining the others in the hotel's foyer, Alec cautioned Claude to keep their conversation to himself.

As the passengers reboarded the double-decker, Paige noticed Alec's smile and asked, "Did you get what you need?"

Alec beamed. "I just have to find physical proof now."

After having a light meal at the Lido buffet, Alec and Paige joined both chapters of the ACA in the Explorer's Club for drinks. Since none of the caterers were persons of interest in Irwin's death, Alec enjoyed the farewell party festivities.

On previous occasions, Alec had been forced to round up suspects and tell them when they were to be interviewed by the police. This case was different. Upon giving Nicola Campbell the latest information, she only requested to see Bella Valentino, Claude Bourdain, Harold Zuma, and, of course, Faith Rossi.

Bella, who had booked a back-to-back cruise to spend extra time with Claude, was amenable to coming to the Hudson Room at nine the following morning. Claude promised to be on hand by nine-thirty.

With nothing else on his mind, Alec celebrated with Derek, Gail, and their fellow caterers. The party ended all too soon, and Paige reminded Alec, "You have to get up early tomorrow and meet Nicola at 7:30 AM."

Winking, Alec responded, "I'll call it a night if you let me scrub your back in the tub."

Paige complied with a smile.

CHAPTER EIGHTEEN

▼

"Mist Covered Mountains"
Words & Music by John Cameron.
Genre: Gaelic Folk Song, Composed in1856

Tuesday Morning—12th of August

Alec silenced the alarm on his cell phone and jumped out of bed, wearing a grin. He had a good night's sleep and was raring to go. Paige moved at a slower pace as she got ready to see her family off the ship at 9:00 AM.

After shaving and showering, Alec dressed and gulped down a cup of black coffee. When Paige offered him some breakfast, he turned it down and said, "I'll probably have something with Nicola."

With a mischievous smile, she responded, "Nicola, is it now? You'd better not abscond with her to Juneau!"

Alec kissed his wife warmly and promised, "I'll visit you at the Future Cruise Desk when the police leave."

Alec dashed out of the cabin moments later and set off for the crew entrance to meet the deputy chief and her contact at the Seattle Homicide Department. Alec had to wait ten minutes and was thrilled when he finally spotted them with several forensic specialists.

Deputy Chief Campbell introduced Alec to Detective Tom Morgan and remarked, "Without the help of Mr. DunBarton, I doubt we would have gotten this far."

Turning to Alec, she resumed, "I'd like the forensics team to inspect Ms. Rossi's cabin first. I have the proper warrant. Do you know her current whereabouts on the ship?"

Alec replied, "The cruise director is at her desk, and the room steward will be on hand to unlock her quarters."

From there, Alec led the group to Faith's cabin on A Deck. As promised, the steward was nearby and let the forensics team into the room. The head technician promised to contact Morgan upon finding anything of note.

Alec then took Nicola and Morgan to the Hudson Room, which he had stocked with a coffee urn and assorted pastries. As Morgan set up the audio-visual equipment, Nicola helped herself to coffee and a chocolate croissant.

It allowed Alec to renew his acquaintance with the deputy chief and recapture some of the comradery they'd shared in Juneau. Although Alec didn't think she'd serenade him again, he was happy to hear her Glaswegian accent.

When the equipment was up and running, Alec gave them *his* taped statement. It included background info on Claude, how Faith dealt with Irwin's physical assault, the resulting pregnancy, and her broken engagement. Detective Morgan was surprised to hear how much Alec had uncovered in his investigation.

Alec had just finished his statement when a light knock sounded on the Hudson Room's closed door. It was Bella, along with Claude Bourdain. After kissing Bella's forehead, the executive chef informed Alec, "I'll be in the hall till you're ready for me."

Bella took her place at a table, and Nicola Campbell asked her at what time she saw Faith outside the gym, how she behaved, and whether she had anything in her hands. The caterer had to cast her mind back to answer her last question and replied, "I think she had a tote bag." When asked about her relationship with the cruise director, Bella reported, "She was rather rude to me at the culinary trivia game. Later, Claude told me about their past."

"Did you ever see Faith Rossi with Mr. Irwin?" she followed.

Bella shook her head and answered, "I didn't, but I can understand why she might have given him a wide berth. He was a menace and always seemed to leave destruction in his wake. I could have killed him myself on several occasions. I still don't know if he had anything to do with Tony's death."

Bourdain was called next and confirmed everything Alec had related earlier. Nicola advised that he and Bella would be required to sign a written statement and possibly testify in court. Appearing forlorn, Claude declared, "I blame the steroids that Bob took. Before he got into all the bodybuilding crap, he was a pretty nice guy."

Alec, less charitable, wondered whether he was always a nasty character and the performance-enhancing drugs made it worse. Those musings were interrupted when Tom Morgan received a call from the chief forensics officer.

Nicola and Alec listened to his one-sided remarks. It was well worth the wait. Upon ending the call, Morgan announced, "The team found a few hypodermic needles and two vials of potassium chloride. She also had a folded hiking cane, masking tape, and some books on suicide. The team has finished and will be returning to headquarters with them, her laptop, and cell phone."

Over the next twenty minutes, the threesome discussed how to handle Faith Rossi's upcoming arrest. It was decided to bring her in next, followed by Security Chief Zuma.

Alec escorted Nicola and Morgan to the cruise director's office. Faith didn't seem upset at seeing Alec with the strangers and asked, "Are you from the police?"

Both officers showed their badges, and Nicola had her stand up as she pronounced:

You have the right to remain silent. Anything you say can and will be used against you in a court of law. You have the right to speak to an attorney, and to have an attorney present during any questioning. If you cannot afford a lawyer, one will be provided for you at government expense.

Despite being given a Miranda Warning, Faith expressed a desire to tell her story. She followed Alec and the others to the Hudson Room to provide a recorded statement. Alec wasn't surprised that she was ready to confess.

Once seated before the audio-visual equipment, Nicola asked, "When did you first learn that Robert Irwin was on board the ship?"

Shrugging, she began, "It was the night I killed him. I saw Bob leave the Culinary Arts Center after the executive chef's dinner. I didn't know he was on the Pegasus or a member of the American Catering Association. He looked as arrogant as ever."

"Did he recognize you?" Nicola probed.

Faith shook her head, "Not then. When I realized he was on his way to the fitness center, I stopped by my cabin to pick up a syringe of potassium chloride, masking tape, and my hiking stick.

"In order to get away with his murder, I knew I'd have to disable the surveillance camera by the gym's entrance. When the fitness instructor left, I saw my chance. It took seconds to place tape on the camera lens.

When I confronted Robert, he just looked at me with a blank expression. He resumed exercising with his back to me and didn't regard me as a threat. It was easy to inject the KCL into his neck. If I had to do it again, I would have aimed higher on his hairline."

Turning to Alec, she declared, "You and the doctor noticed the puncture wound, didn't you? And Claude's female friend saw me hanging around the gym. I did a public service. You should be congratulating me!"

Alec had questions on the tip of his tongue and received a nod from Nicola to voice them. Delicately, he asked, "Why did you have hypodermic needles and potassium chloride vials in your cabin? You stated that you weren't aware of Irwin's presence on the Pegasus until you actually saw him."

Faith, looking more miserable, explained, "I planned to kill myself a few months ago. I had been waiting for the right day to go through with it. Now, I'm glad I put it off. The depression that has been crippling me is gone. I don't mind going to prison. After what I've experienced, it will feel like a vacation."

Alec's second question concerned the fitness center's cameras. Casually, he asked, "Did Harold Zuma help you in any way?"

Faith seemed surprised by the question and promised he had nothing to do with the murder. Since breaking up with him, she had tried to have as little to do with him as possible.

With tears in her eyes, she added, "Harold encouraged me to see a therapist. I never told him about my past. He only knew I was prone to depression and felt I should talk to an impartial person.

After Faith completed her statement, Detective Morgan placed handcuffs on her and escorted her from the ship to an awaiting police car. While he was gone, Security Chief Zuma barged into the room.

Anger plainly showing on his face, he cursed, "What the hell happened? Faith was just taken off the ship in handcuffs. She couldn't have killed Robert Irwin. She didn't even know him."

Though Detective Morgan had not yet returned, Nicola turned on the recording equipment and questioned Zuma about the gym's surveillance cameras and what he knew of Faith's past. He was interviewed for twenty minutes and then released.

Both Alec and Nicola concluded he had nothing to do with Irwin's murder. If that changed, she agreed to have the Juneau police re-interview him when the ship was back in Alaskan waters.

While Nicola was packing the equipment, Morgan returned and thanked Alec for his diligence. The threesome parted at the pier, and as Alec watched Nicola go, he realized he was homesick for Scotland.

Alec visited Paige shortly afterward. She was back at her Future Cruise Desk. New passengers were on board for the ship's next voyage to Alaska. People were lined up at the Front Desk with questions about their cabins and the upcoming sailing.

From her demeanor, Alec could see she was downhearted and asked, "Were you able to see off the family?"

Paige confessed, "I did, but it was bittersweet. Dad made reservations for Aunt Irena to revisit California this Christmas. They were content, and Derek and Gail appeared eager to return home with Oliver. The boy gave me a wet kiss, and before I knew it, they were gone."

Alec hugged her, hoping to make her feel better. As a smile partially returned to her face, she recalled, "The captain came by. He wants to see you."

Not wanting to keep Charles Stewart waiting, Alec promised to join Paige at noon to grab a quick meal.

Alec was not concerned about the captain's summons. He expected that Stewart just wanted an update on Faith's arrest and what part, if any, the security chief played in the murder. From past experience, Alec knew that Stewart disliked having the Pegasus in the news and partly held Alec responsible whenever unsavory problems popped up. He once called him a "bad penny."

The captain ushered Alec into his ready room with a bland expression and had him take a seat at his table. He didn't seem unduly annoyed as Alec reported how the police interviews went. He even smiled upon hearing that Harold Zuma wasn't suspected of aiding Faith Rossi.

Alec did *not* expect to hear Stewart's following words. Without emotion, he said, "This morning, I heard from the captain of the Centaurus and his security chief. They have requested your presence on their ship. They want you to audit the books of their controller, who deserted the ship without permission.

Stewart continued, "You, of course, have been permitted to bring Paige. She'll be asked to stand in at their Future Cruise Desk. The Centaurus is currently following its British Isles itinerary. The thirteen-day cruise from Dover includes stops in Scotland and Ireland."

Alec smiled inwardly and asked, "When do you want us to go?"

"Now," the captain responded. "Security Chief Tucker has arranged for you and your wife to catch a British Air nonstop flight from Seattle to Gatwick. He will email you further details. I trust you'll have enough time to pack and get your papers in order. Here's the info.

Alec took the slip of paper from his outstretched hand. After noting the flight was scheduled to leave at 7:40 PM and international passengers were expected to be at the airport three hours early, Alec realized he couldn't dally.

He thanked the captain, and Stewart's smile said he was pleased to see the back of him. As Alec made his way to Paige, he sang,

Oh, roe, soon shall I see them, oh,
Hee-roe, see them, oh see them.
Oh, roe, soon shall I see them,
the mist covered mountains of home!

There shall I visit the place of my birth.
They'll give me a welcome, the warmest on earth.
So loving and kind, full of music and mirth,
the sweet-sounding language of home.

There shall I gaze on the mountains again.
On the fields, and the hills, and the birds in the glen.
With people of courage beyond human ken!
In the haunts of the deer I will roam.

Hail to the mountains with summits of blue!
To the glens with their meadows of sunshine and dew.
To the women and the men ever constant and true,
Ever ready to welcome one home!

Back at the cruise desk, Alec jubilantly kissed Paige until she begged him to stop. Concerned he had lost his mind, she asked, "Are you okay?"

Full of joy, he replied, "Sign off your computer. We must eat, pack our bags, say goodbye to Douglas and Regina, and take a cab to the airport. We've been invited to join the Centaurus and cruise around the British Islands."

Dumbstruck, she asked, "Was someone murdered?"

Alec replied with a firm *no* but added, "I've been asked to investigate a possible embezzlement. That's nearly as good as a murder!"

EPILOGUE

**Wednesday Morning
13th of August
8:00 AM**

The plane's cabin lights came on at 8:00 AM sharp. Seeing Paige's eyes open, Alec asked, "Did you get any sleep?"

"Not much," she groaned. "I'm glad we don't have to board the Centaurus until the sixteenth. It will give us a chance to acclimate to the time difference."

Alec agreed and brought down the seat-back table in readiness for breakfast. Paige followed suit. The aroma of the coffee, wafting down the aisle, was just what Alec needed to start the day. He, too, had just caught a few minutes here and there.

Although they were seated in economy, their breakfast turned out to be better than the one they last had in first class. With gusto, Alec dug into his meal of scrambled eggs, hash browns, fried tomatoes, and sautéed mushrooms. With their English breakfast, they were also given a hot cinnamon roll, a flaky croissant, sliced fruit, and vanilla yogurt.

Over a second cup of coffee, Alec reviewed the email he had received from Benjamin Tucker III. The man was a good friend and also the current security chief of the Centaurus.

Paige looked over Alec's shoulder as he reread the message:

Subj: Travel Info and Hotel Accommodation
Date: 12th of August, 6:21:51 PM BST
From: BTucker@Centaurus.com
To: AlecDunBarton@aol.com

Alec,

I've just gotten permission from Captain Stewart to allow you and Paige to join the Centaurus. Right now, the ship is on its thirteen-day British Isles cruise. We'll be in Cork tomorrow and return to Dover on the sixteenth. At that time, you'll be able to board.

As you may or may not know, our former controller, Sam Warren, left the ship on the eleventh while we were docked in Douglas, Isle of Man. When he didn't return by 6:00 PM, I checked his cabin and saw that most of his clothes were gone. We believe he took a ferry from Douglas to Liverpool. Since we don't know why he left, we need you to complete an audit of our ship's records.

Because of the short notice, I could only reserve economy seats on a nonstop flight from Seattle. You can pick up the boarding passes from the airport. The flight from Seattle to London will take eleven hours! From Gatwick Airport, you can catch several trains to Dover.

I inserted the ship's itinerary and booked you a Premium King Room with a Sea View at the Voco Clifton Hotel in Folkestone for three nights. They have an agreement with the cruise line and should be able to accommodate all your needs. I understand they have delicious breakfasts. As I recall, you have a healthy appetite and love to eat!

I'll see you in a few days,
BT

Paige was still chuckling at Ben's comment when Alec looked at the Centaurus ports of call. It read:

Centaurus Itinerary

13-Day British Isles Cruise
Dover to Dover

Date	Day	Port of Call	Arrival	Departure
16-Aug	Sat	Dover, England		6:00 PM
17-Aug	Sun	*At Sea*		
18-Aug	Mon	Newcastle upon Tyne, England	8:00 AM	5:00 PM
19-Aug	Tue	Invergordon, (Inverness), Scotland	9:00 AM	6:00 PM
20-Aug	Wed	Lerwick, Shetland Islands, Scotland	8:00 AM	4:00 PM
21-Aug	Thu	Stornoway, Isle of Lewis, Scotland	8:00 AM	5:00 PM
22-Aug	Fri	Belfast, Northern Ireland	8:00 AM	6:00 PM
23-Aug	Sat	Greenock, (Glasgow), Scotland	8:00 AM	6:00 PM
24-Aug	Sun	Douglas, Isle of Man, England	8:00 AM	6:00 PM
25-Aug	Mon	*At Sea*		
26-Aug	Tue	Cobb, (Cork), Ireland	7:00 AM	5:00 PM
27-Aug	Wed	Dun Laoghaire, (Dublin), Ireland	7:00 AM	5:00 PM
28-Aug	Thu	*At Sea*		
29-Aug	Fri	Dover, England	7:00 AM	

After reviewing the places Alec had been to while living in the UK, the couple discussed the sites they wished to visit together. Alec's great-great-grandparent, Malcolm DunBarton, had hailed from Dunbartonshire, an agricultural district northwest of Glasgow. He helped build the Cutty Sark tea clipper in the late 1860s and then moved to Inverness to find his way in the world.

Noting that the Centaurus was scheduled to stop in Inverness on the nineteenth, Paige said, "I hope we can spend the day with William and Roddy. Your cousins may be too busy at the DunBarton Inn to have time for us."

"I'm sure they'll greet us with open arms," Alec replied. "We last saw them when the hotel hosted a writers' weekend, and the book critic was beheaded with a paper cutter."

Paige shivered, "Please, don't remind me."

"At least," Alec recalled, "It was all forgotten by the time we wed in November. The inn looked gorgeous, and I sang, 'You Had Me from Hello' after we exchanged vows."

The DunBartons continued to reminisce for a while, and then Alec confessed, "I need to tell you something."

Momentarily alarmed, Paige listened as Alec admitted, "I called my parents while you were packing our suitcases on the Pegasus. I gave them our flight details, and they plan to pick us up at Gatwick Airport. I couldn't see us taking a train and cab after being on an eleven-hour flight. They've been asking to get together with us since we sailed on the Pisces' repositioning cruise."

Paige sighed in response and confirmed, "Your mother was friendlier to me on that trip and subsequent vacation in Florida. I hope she remembers we're not at odds anymore. Your dad, of course, has always been charming."

Alec agreed, "On your first meeting with my mother, she tried to break off our engagement. I wouldn't have been able to forgive her had she succeeded. Instead of returning to America, you hung in and just changed hotel rooms."

Laughing now, Paige recalled, "You and Roddy opened that secret passageway between your bedroom and mine. It was very exciting."

Alec grinned. "I was like a dog with a bone, trying to get to you. Let's hope my English mother no longer behaves like a territorial and excitable British terrier."

Paige muttered, "Amen."

Deliteful Dessert Recipes
100 to 200 Calorie Snacks

———————▼———————

Includes:

Almond Cashew Cookies: *164 calories each*
Apple Cake Squares: *132 per portion*
Banana Nut Muffins: *164 calories each*
Blueberry Cream Tarts: *131 calories each*
Carrot Cake Squares: *149 calories per portion*
Cherry Crumb Tarts: *184 calories each*
Chocolate Brownies, *102 calories per portion*
Cranberry Pumpkin Muffins: *163 calories each*
Irish Soda Breads: *176 calories each*
Key Lime Cheesecakes: *159 calories each*
Lemon Ricotta Tarts: *168 calories each*
Oatmeal Raisin Cookies: *108 calories each*
Peach Turnovers: *141 calories each*
Peanut Butter Cookies: *169 calories each*
Pecan Blondies: *147 calories per portion*
Pumpkin Pies: *136 calories each*
Rhubarb Crumble: *169 calories per portion*
Strawberry Shortcakes: *176/156 per portion*

Almond Cashew Cookies
Makes Twelve (two and a half inches)

<u>Ingredients</u>
>   ¾ cup cashew butter
>   ½ cup and 2 tablespoons light brown sugar, firmly packed
>   ¾ cup whole wheat flour
>   1 large egg
>   ¼ teaspoon almond extract
>   additional flour or an egg white, if necessary

Preheat the oven to 350°F, and line a cookie sheet with parchment paper. In a medium bowl, mix together all the ingredients.

The dough may be sticky or dry depending on the cashew butter brand. Add additional flour if it is too wet or an egg white if it is too dry.

Form the dough into 12 balls and place them on the cookie sheet. Flatten to about ⅓ to ½ inch thick with additional flour, if necessary.

Bake 11 to 13 minutes or until the cookies are lightly browned on the edges and set in the center. Cool on the cookie sheet for 5 minutes before transferring it to a wire rack. Cookies can be frozen until ready to thaw and eat.

Nutrition Facts for Almond Cashew Cookies

Ingredients	Calories	Sodium	Carbs	Fiber	Protein
Cashew Butter	1140	390	60	6	24
Light Brown Sugar	450	0	120	0	0
Whole Wheat Flour	300	0	63	12	12
Large Egg	74	70	0	0	6
Almond Extract	3	0	0	0	0
Totals:	1967	460	243	18	42
1 Cashew Cookie	164	38	20	1.5	3.5

****

Apple Cake Squares
Makes Sixteen (2-inch by 2-inch squares)

<u>Ingredients</u>

 1 cup whole wheat flour
 ⅓ cup all-purpose flour
 ⅓ cup granulated sugar
 ¼ cup brown sugar, firmly packed
 1 teaspoon cinnamon
 ½ teaspoon baking powder
 ½ teaspoon baking soda
  2 eggs, lightly beaten
  ½ cup unsweetened applesauce
  ⅓ cup canola oil
   4 cups apples, unpeeled and cut into ½-inch by ½-inch pieces

Preheat the oven to 325°F. Grease and line an 8x8-square baking pan with parchment paper. In a large bowl, combine the flours, sugar, cinnamon, baking powder, and baking soda.

Add the beaten eggs, unsweetened applesauce, and canola oil. Mix well and fold in the apples. Pour the batter into the prepared pan and bake for 40 to 45 minutes or until the apples are tender.

Cool on a wire rack. The apple cake squares are best served warm. They freeze well and can be served later.

Nutrition Facts for Apple Cake Squares

Ingredients	Calories	Sodium	Carbs	Fiber	Protein
Whole Wheat Flour	400	0	84	12	16
All-Purpose Flour	147	0	31	1	4
Granulated Sugar	258	0	66	0	0
Dark Brown Sugar	180	0	48	0	0
Eggs	148	140	1	0	13
Canola Oil	642	0	0	0	0
Unsweetened Applesauce	52	2	14	1.5	0
Apples	284	4	76	13	1.5
Totals:	2111	146	320	27.5	34.5

Apple Cake (2" by 2")	132	9	20	2	2

****

Banana Nut Muffins
Makes Twelve

<u>Ingredients</u>
1 cup overripe bananas (3 large), mashed
4 tablespoons butter, melted and cooled
⅔ cup whole wheat flour
⅔ cup all-purpose flour
½ cup granulated sugar
1 teaspoon baking soda
½ teaspoon baking powder
1 large egg, beaten
½ cup unsweetened apple sauce
1½ teaspoons vanilla extract
⅓ cup pecans, finely chopped

Preheat the oven to 350°F. Grease and flour a muffin tin or insert cupcake liners. In a small bowl, mash the bananas, keeping one cup for the recipe. Melt the butter and set aside to cool.

In a large bowl, combine the flours, sugar, baking soda, and baking powder, and mix together. Stir in the mashed banana, beaten egg, applesauce, melted butter, and vanilla extract. Fold in the coarsely chopped walnuts. The batter will be thick.

Bake the muffins for 25 to 30 minutes or until the cake tester comes out clean and the banana nut muffins are golden brown. Cool in the pan for a few minutes before moving to a wire rack. The muffins freeze well and can be enjoyed at a later time.

Nutrition Facts for Banana Nut Muffins

Ingredients	Calories	Sodium	Carbs	Fiber	Protein
Bananas	200	2	51	6	2.5
Salted Butter	408	328	0	0	0
Whole Wheat Flour	266	0	56	8	11
All-Purpose Flour	293	0	61	2	8
Granulated Sugar	387	0	100	0	0
Unsweetened Applesauce	52	2	14	1.5	0
Large Egg	74	70	0	0	6
Vanilla Extract	18	0	0	0	0
Pecans	274	0	5	4	4
Totals:	1972	402	287	21.5	31.5

| 1 Banana Nut Muffin | 164 | 34 | 24 | 2 | 3 |

Blueberry Cream Pies
Makes Twelve

<u>Ingredients</u>
¾ cup graham cracker crumbs
1 tablespoon granulated sugar
4 tablespoons butter, melted
1½ cups fresh blueberries
1 cup light sour cream
1 large egg, beaten
¼ cup light brown sugar, firmly packed
½ tablespoon cornstarch
1 teaspoon vanilla extract

Preheat the oven to 375°F. Insert 12 cupcake liners into a muffin tin. In a small bowl, mix the graham cracker crumbs, sugar, and melted butter until the mixture adheres together. Spoon the mixture into the muffin liners and press down with the bottom of a glass. Bake for 5 minutes or until light brown. Allow them to cool on a wire rack and reduce the oven to 350°F.

Divide the blueberries into 12 portions and place onto the parbaked crust. In a large bowl, mix together the sour cream, beaten egg, brown sugar, cornstarch, and vanilla extract. Spoon a few tablespoons of the cream filling onto the blueberries and smooth with a butter knife.

Bake for an additional 25 to 30 minutes or until the filling is set and a cake tester, inserted in the center, comes out clean. Cool on a wire rack and refrigerate an hour before eating.

Nutrition Facts for Blueberry Cream Pies

Ingredients	Calories	Sodium	Carbs	Fiber	Protein
Graham Cracker Crumbs	390	630	69	3	6
Granulated Sugar	45	0	12	0	0
Salted Butter	408	328	0	0	0
Blueberries	124	1	32	5	1.5
Light Sour Cream	320	200	24	0	8
Large Egg	74	70	0	0	6
Light Brown Sugar	180	0	48	0	0
Cornstarch/Vanilla	27	0	4	0	0
Totals:	1568	1229	189	8	21.5

| 1 Blueberry Cream Pie | 131 | 102 | 16 | 1 | 2 |

Carrot Cake Squares
Makes Sixteen (2-inch by 2-inch squares)

<u>Ingredients</u>

1⅓ cups wholewheat flour
⅔ cup dark brown sugar, firmly packed
2 teaspoons cinnamon
1¼ teaspoon baking soda
3 large eggs, beaten
⅓ cup canola oil
⅓ cup unsweetened applesauce
1½ teaspoons vanilla extract
1⅓ cups grated carrots
⅓ cup unsweetened crushed pineapple
¼ cup walnuts, finely chopped
2 tablespoons unsweetened coconut

Preheat the oven to 350°F. Grease an 8x8 glass baking dish and line it with a rectangular piece of parchment paper. In a large mixing bowl, combine the flour, sugar, cinnamon, and baking soda. In another bowl, mix the eggs, canola oil, unsweetened applesauce, and vanilla extract.

Stir the wet ingredients into the dry and mix until blended. Add the grated carrots, drained pineapple (no juice), walnuts, and unsweetened coconut. Pour the mixture into the prepared baking dish.

Bake for 25 to 30 minutes or until the cake tester inserted into the center comes out clean and the cake springs back when touched. Cool on a rack and remove the parchment paper before cutting into 16 squares.

Nutrition Facts for Carrot Cake Squares

Ingredients	Calories	Sodium	Carbs	Fiber	Protein
Whole Wheat Flour	520	0	109	16	21
Dark Brown Suger	540	0	144	0	0
Canola Oil	642	0	0	0	0
Large Eggs	222	210	1	0	19
Unsweetened Applesauce	35	2	9	1	0
Carrots	60	101	14	4	1
Unsweetened Pineapple	70	0	16	0	0
Walnuts	200	0	4	2	5
Unsweetened Coconut	70	0	3	2	1
Totals:	**2359**	**313**	**300**	**25**	**47**
Carrot Cake (2" by 2")	**149**	**20**	**19**	**1.5**	**3**

Cherry Crumb Tarts
Makes Nine

Ingredients

1 cup whole wheat flour
¼ cup light brown sugar
1 teaspoon cinnamon
6 tablespoons cold butter
14.5-ounce can of red tart cherries
⅓ cup granulated sugar
1 tablespoon cornstarch

Preheat the oven to 350°F. Grease eight compartments of a muffin tin or line with cupcake papers. In a small bowl, combine the flour, sugar, and cinnamon. Cut in the butter and work with your fingers until the mixture is crumbly.

Pat half the tart mixture into the bottom of eight muffin tin compartments. Save the remaining crumbs for the topping. Bake the base for 6 to 8 minutes or until light brown.

Drain the liquid from the can of cherries and pour ½ cup into a small saucepan. Stir in the sugar and cornstarch, and heat until the mixture thickens. Turn off the heat and add the cherries to the thickened sauce. Mash the cherries slightly so the sauce seeps into the pitted cherries. Set aside to cool.

To assemble, place a few tablespoons of the cherry mixtures into each tart. Sprinkle the remaining crumb mixture over the cherries. Bake an additional 10 to 12 minutes or until the topping has begun to brown. Cool on a wire rack and refrigerate an hour before eating. The cherry crumb tarts can be frozen and enjoyed later.

Nutrition Facts for Cherry Crumb Tarts

Ingredients	Calories	Sodium	Carbs	Fiber	Protein
Whole Wheat Flour	400	0	84	12	16
Light Brown Sugar	180	0	48	0	0
Salted Butter	610	492	0	0	1
Red Tart Cherries	180	30	42	6	3
Granulated Sugar	258	0	66	0	0
Cornstarch	30	0	7	0	0
Totals:	1658	522	247	18	20

| 1 Cherry Crumb Tart | 184 | 58 | 27 | 2 | 2 |

Chocolate Brownies
Makes Sixteen (2-inch by 2-inch squares)

<u>Ingredients</u>
¾ cup whole wheat flour
½ cup unsweetened cocoa powder
½ cup granulated sugar
⅓ cup dark brown sugar, firmly packed
½ teaspoon baking powder
½ teaspoon baking soda
½ cup unsweetened applesauce
¼ cup canola oil
1 large egg, lightly beaten
1 teaspoon vanilla extract
¼ teaspoon almond extract

Preheat the oven to 350°F. Grease an 8x8 glass baking dish and line it with a rectangular piece of parchment paper.

In a large mixing bowl, combine the flour, cocoa powder, sugars, baking powder, and baking soda. Add the applesauce, melted butter, beaten egg, vanilla, and almond extract. Mix until blended. Pour in the prepared baking dish.

Bake for 20 to 25 minutes until the center has risen and the edges have set. The brownies will firm up as they thoroughly cool on a wire rack.

Remove the parchment paper before cutting it into 16 pieces. Leftovers can be frozen and enjoyed later.

Nutrition Facts for Chocolate Brownies

Ingredients	Calories	Sodium	Carbs	Fiber	Protein
Whole Wheat Flour	300	0	63	9	12
Unsweetened Cocoa Powder	80	0	24	12	8
Granulated Sugar	387	0	100	0	0
Dark Brown Sugar	240	0	64	0	0
Unsweetened Applesauce	52	0	14	1.5	0
Canola Oil	494	0	0	0	0
Large Egg	74	70	0	0	6
Vanilla Extract	12	0	1	0	0
Totals:	1639	70	266	22.5	26

Choc. Brownie (2" by 2")	102	4	17	1.5	1.5

Cranberry Pumpkin Muffins
Makes Twelve

<u>Ingredients</u>
1 cup whole wheat flour
⅓ cup all-purpose flour
½ cup granulated sugar
2 teaspoons pumpkin pie spice
1 teaspoon baking soda
½ teaspoon baking powder
⅔ cup canned pure pumpkin
2 eggs, lightly beaten
⅓ cup canola oil
½ cup unsweetened applesauce
3 tablespoons juice from fresh orange
¼ cup dried craisins (50% less sugar), cut in half

Preheat the oven to 350°F. Grease and flour a muffin tin or insert cupcake liners. In a large bowl, combine the flours, sugar, pumpkin pie spice, baking soda, and baking powder.

Add the pumpkin, beaten eggs, oil, applesauce, and juice from an orange. Mix until blended. Fold in the dried cranberries.

Spoon the batter into the prepared pan. Bake for 25 to 30 minutes or until the cake tester inserted in the cracks comes out clean. Let the muffins cool on a wire rack. The muffins freeze well and can be served at a later time.

Nutrition Facts for Cranberry Pumpkin Muffins

Ingredients	Calories	Sodium	Carbs	Fiber	Protein
Whole Wheat Flour	400	0	84	12	16
All-Purpose Flour	146	0	30	1	4
Granulated Sugar	387	0	100	0	0
Pumpkin Pie Spice	12	2	2	1	0
Canned Pumpkin	53	10	13	4	1
Eggs	148	140	0	0	13
Canola Oil	642	0	0	0	0
Unsweetened Applesauce	52	0	14	1.5	0
Orange Juice	21	0	5	0	0
Craisins	100	0	33	10	0
Totals:	1961	152	281	29.5	34

1 Cran-Pumpkin Muffin	163	13	23	2.5	3

Irish Soda Bread
Makes Ten

Ingredients

    1 cup whole wheat flour
    1 cup all-purpose flour
    ¼ cup granulated sugar
    ½ teaspoon baking soda
    ½ teaspoon cream of tartar
    4 tablespoons salted butter
        ⅔ cup low-fat buttermilk
        1 large egg, lightly beaten
        ¼ cup raisins
        2 teaspoons caraway seeds

Preheat the oven to 350°F. Line a cookie sheet with parchment paper. In a large bowl, mix together the flours, sugar, baking soda, and cream of tartar. Cut in the butter until the mixture resembles cornmeal.

Add the buttermilk and beaten egg all at once. Stir with a fork until just blended. Add the raisins and caraway seeds. Knead about 10 times with additional flour until it adheres together.

Divide the dough into 10 portions, form in small balls, and transfer to the cookie sheet. With a knife, cut a small X on the top, about a ¼-inch deep so you can see four evenly sized quarters.

Bake for 14 to 16 minutes or until a cake tester comes out clean. Cool on a wire rack. Leftovers can be frozen and warmed later in the oven or microwave.

Nutrition Facts for Irish Soda Muffins

Ingredients	Calories	Sodium	Carbs	Fiber	Protein
Whole Wheat Flour	407	6	87	15	16
White Flour	440	0	92	3	12
Granulated Sugar	194	0	50	0	0
Baking Soda	0	630	0	0	0
Salted Butter	408	328	0	0	9
Low Fat Buttermilk	90	83	9	0	6
Large Egg	80	62	0	0	6
Raisins	120	0	32	1	1
Caraway Seeds	21	0	3	2	1
Totals:	1760	1109	273	21	51

1 Irish Soda Bread	176	111	27	2	5

Key Lime Cheesecakes (Unbaked)
Makes Nine

Ingredients

10 tablespoons graham cracker crumbs
3 tablespoons salted butter, melted
¼ cup hot water
2 teaspoons unflavored gelatin
4 ounces reduced-fat cream cheese, softened
⅓ cup granulated sugar
5.3 ounces Dannon, Light & Fit, Lime Greek yogurt
2 tablespoons fresh lime juice
1 teaspoon fresh lime zest
1 cup frozen whipped dessert topping, thawed
decorate with extra lime zest

Insert nine cupcake liners into a muffin tin. Mix the gelatin with hot water and set it aside. In a small bowl, mix the graham cracker crumbs and melted butter until the mixture adheres together. Spoon the mixture into the muffin liners and press down with the bottom of a glass. Chill in the refrigerator while preparing the filling.

In a medium bowl, cream the cream cheese with the granulated sugar until smooth. Add the yogurt, gelatin mixture, lime juice, and zest. Stir until the mixture is creamy. Fold in the thawed, whipped dessert topping.

Remove the muffin tin from the refrigerator and spoon a few tablespoons of the lime mixture on top of the graham cracker base. Smooth with a knife and dust with additional lime zest. Refrigerate for at least three hours. The mini cheesecakes can be frozen.

Nutrition Facts for Key Lime Cheesecakes

Ingredients	Calories	Sodium	Carbs	Fiber	Protein
Unflavored Gelatin	20	0	0	0	4
Graham Cracker Crumbs	300	475	55	1	6
Salted Butter	306	273	0	0	0
Reduced Fat Cream Cheese	280	420	8	0	8
Granulated Suger	258	0	66	0	0
Key Lime Greek Yogurt	80	45	9	1	12
Lime Juice/Zest	8	0	0	0	0
Whipped Dessert Topping	200	0	24	0	0
Totals:	1452	1213	162	2	30

| 1 Key Lime Cheesecake | 159 | 135 | 18 | 0 | 3 |

Lemon Ricotta Tarts
Makes Nine

<u>Ingredients</u>
    ⅔ cup whole wheat flour
    1 tablespoon granulated sugar
    3 tablespoons salted butter, melted
        12 ounces low-fat ricotta cheese (1⅓ cups)
        ⅓ cup half and half
        ½ cup granulated sugar
        2 large eggs, lightly beaten
        3 tablespoons fresh lemon juice
        1 tablespoon fresh lemon zest

Insert nine cupcake liners into a muffin tin. Preheat the oven to 375°F. In a small bowl, mix the whole wheat flour, sugar, and melted butter until the mixture adheres together. Spoon the mixture into the muffin liners and press down with the bottom of a floured glass. Bake for about 5 minutes or until lightly browned. Allow them to cool, and reduce the oven temperature to 350°F.

In a medium bowl, combine the ricotta, half and half, sugar, beaten eggs, lemon juice, and lemon zest. Mix well. Spoon a few tablespoons onto the prebaked crust. Smooth out the cheese mixture with a knife.

Bake for an additional 22 to 27 minutes or until the filling is set and a cake tester inserted in the center comes out clean. Cool on a wire rack and refrigerate for an hour before eating. The lemon ricotta tarts can be frozen and enjoyed later.

Nutrition Facts for Lemon Ricotta Tarts

Ingredients	Calories	Sodium	Carbs	Fiber	Protein
Whole Wheat Flour	266	0	56	8	11
Granulated Sugar	45	0	12	0	0
Salted Butter	300	475	55	1	6
Low Fat Ricotta Cheese	233	373	21	5.5	32
Half and Half	107	32	3	0	2
Granulated Sugar	387	0	100	0	0
Large Eggs	148	140	0	1	13
Lemon Juice/Zest	15	0	5	1	0
Totals:	1501	1020	252	16.5	64
1 Lemon Ricotta Tart	168	113	28	2	7

Oatmeal Raisin Cookies
Makes Twelve (two and a half inches)

Ingredients

⅔ cup quick-cooking oats
½ cup whole wheat flour
½ cup dark brown sugar, firmly packed
½ teaspoon baking powder
½ teaspoon cinnamon
1 large egg
3 tablespoons salted butter, melted
1 teaspoon vanilla extract
¼ teaspoon almond extract
⅓ cup raisins

Preheat the oven to 350°F, and line a cookie sheet with parchment paper. In a medium bowl, mix together the quick-cooking oats, whole-wheat flour, brown sugar, baking powder, and cinnamon.

In a separate bowl, whisk together the egg, melted butter, vanilla, and almond extract. Stir the liquids into the dry ingredients until mixed. Fold in the raisins. The cookie dough will be sticky.

Drop the dough by heaping tablespoons onto the prepared cookie sheet. Bake for 11-13 minutes or until the cookies are lightly browned on the edges.

The cookies may look partially undone, but they will set upon cooling. Leave them on the cookie sheet for about 5 minutes before transferring to a wire rack. Cookies can be frozen and enjoyed later.

Nutrition Facts for Oatmeal Raisin Cookies

Ingredients	Calories	Sodium	Carbs	Fiber	Protein
Quick-Cooking Oats	200	0	36	6	7
Whole Wheat Flour	200	3	42	6	8
Dark Brown Sugar	360	0	96	0	0
Large Egg	74	70	0	0	6
Salted Butter	306	246	0	0	9
Vanilla Extract	12	0	0	0	0
Raisins	144	0	38	2	1
Totals:	**1296**	**319**	**212**	**14**	**31**

1 Oatmeal Cookie	108	27	18	1	2.5

Peach Turnovers
Makes Nine

<u>Ingredients</u>
>1 sheet (17.3-ounce frozen puff pastry package)
>¼ cup all-purpose flour (for rolling)
>1½ cups unpeeled peaches, diced small
>1 tablespoon firmly packed dark brown sugar
>½ tablespoon cornstarch
>½ teaspoon cinnamon
>¼ teaspoon almond extract
>egg wash (beaten egg with 1 tablespoon water)
>2 tablespoons powdered sugar

Defrost one sheet of puff pastry from a 17.3-ounce package and thaw for about 50 minutes in the refrigerator. Preheat the oven to 400°F, and line a baking sheet with parchment paper.

Cut the unpeeled peaches into ½-inch slices and dice each into four smaller pieces. In a medium bowl, place the peaches, brown sugar, cornstarch, and cinnamon. Mix until the peaches are coated and set aside.

Unfold the sheet of puff pastry from the refrigerator and place it on a floured board, using some of the ¼ cup flour. Roll out the creases so the puff pastry measures 9x9 inches. With a butter knife, cut into nine 3x3-inch squares.

Spoon about a tablespoon of the peach mixture in the center of a square and fold over one corner to form a triangle. Press the open sides down with your fingertips and crimp the edges with the tines of a fork dipped in flour. Repeat with the remaining eight squares.

Place the turnovers on a prepared cookie sheet. Brush the tops of each turnover with the egg wash and prick the tops with a fork to allow the steam to escape. Bake for 15 minutes or until they are puffed, sizzling, and golden brown.

Dust the turnovers with powdered sugar while still warm. The turnovers are best when freshly baked. They can be frozen without sugar and served later with a dusting of powdered sugar. The peach filling can be prepared and refrigerated a day or two before baking.

Nutrition Facts for Peach Turnovers

Ingredients	Calories	Sodium	Carbs	Fiber	Protein
Puff Pastry Sheet	900	840	78	0	12
All Purpose Flour	110	0	23	1	3
Peaches	99	0	24	4	3
Dark Brown Sugar	45	0	12	0	0
Cornstarch	17	0	4	0	0
Egg Wash	37	35	0	0	3
Powdered Sugar	60	0	15	0	0
Totals:	1268	875	156	5	21

1 Peach Turnover	141	97	17	0.5	2

****

Peanut Butter Cookies
Makes Thirteen (two-and-a-half inches)

Ingredients

    ¾ cup peanut butter
    ½ cup and 2 tablespoons light brown sugar, firmly packed
    ¾ cup whole wheat flour
    1 large egg, lightly beaten
    1 teaspoon vanilla extract
        additional flour or an egg white, if necessary

Preheat the oven to 350°F and line a cookie sheet with parchment paper. In a medium bowl, mix together all the ingredients. The dough may be overly sticky or dry, depending on the peanut butter brand. If sticky, add a bit more flour, and if dry, an egg white.

Form the dough into 12 rounds and place them onto the cookie sheet. Press the tines of a floured fork onto each cookie to form a checkerboard pattern.

Bake for 11-13 minutes or until the cookies are lightly browned on the edges. The center will still look soft but will set as it cools. Leave them on the cookie sheet for 5 minutes before transferring to a wire rack. Cookies can be frozen until ready to thaw and eat.

Nutrition Facts for Peanut Butter Cookies

Ingredients	Calories	Sodium	Carbs	Fiber	Protein
Peanut Butter	1200	750	42	9	48
Light Brown Sugar	450	0	120	0	0
Whole Wheat Flour	300	0	63	12	12
Large Egg	74	70	0	0	6
Vanilla Extract	12	0	0	0	0
Totals:	2036	820	225	21	66

1 Peanut Butter Cookie   **169**   **68**   **19**   **2**   **5.5**

****

Pecan Blondies
Makes Sixteen (2-inch by 2-inch)

<u>Ingredients</u>

6 tablespoons salted butter, melted, browned, and cooled
1 cup whole wheat flour
⅔ cup dark brown sugar, firmly packed
½ teaspoon baking powder
½ teaspoon baking soda
½ cup unsweetened applesauce
1 large egg, lightly beaten
1½ teaspoons vanilla extract
⅓ cup pecans, chopped
⅓ cup mini semi-sweet chocolate chips

Preheat the oven to 350°F. Grease and flour an 8x8-inch square pan. Melt the butter in a small saucepan until the milk solids have browned but not burned. Set aside to cool.

In a large bowl, combine the flour, brown sugar, baking powder, and baking soda. Add the melted butter, applesauce, beaten eggs, and vanilla extract. Mix until blended and fold in the chopped pecans and chocolate chips.

Spoon the batter into the pan and smooth the top with a butter knife. Bake for 20 to 25 minutes or until the center is set. The blondies will continue to firm up. Let them cool completely in the pan before cutting them into 16 squares. The blondies freeze well and can be served later.

Nutrition Facts for Pecan Blondies

Ingredients	Calories	Sodium	Carbs	Fiber	Protein
Whole Wheat Flour	400	0	84	12	16
Dark Brown Sugar	480	0	128	0	0
Unsweetened Applesauce	52	3	14	1.5	0
Large Egg	74	70	0	0	6
Salted Butter	612	492	0	0	1
Vanilla Extract	24	0	1	0	0
Semi-Sweet Choc. Chips	443	0	57	6	6
Pecans	274	0	6	4	5
Totals:	2359	565	290	23.5	34

Pecan Blondie (2" by 2")	147	35	18	1.5	2

****

Pumpkin Mini Pies
Makes Ten

Ingredients

¾ cup graham cracker crumbs
1 tablespoon granulated sugar
4 tablespoons salted butter, melted
1½ cups pure pumpkin
2 large eggs, lightly beaten
⅓ cup granulated sugar
2 tablespoons dark brown sugar, firmly packed
½ cup half and half
1½ teaspoons pumpkin pie spice

Insert 12 cupcake liners into a muffin tin. Preheat the oven to 375°F. In a small bowl, mix the cracker crumbs, sugar, and melted butter until the mixture adheres together. Spoon the mixture into the muffin liners and press down with the bottom of a glass. Bake for about 5 minutes or until lightly browned. Let them cool, and reduce the oven temperature to 350°F.

In a large bowl, mix together all the remaining ingredients. Spoon a few tablespoons of the pie filling into each muffin compartment and smooth the top with a butter knife.

Bake for an additional 25 to 30 minutes or until the pumpkin filling is set and a cake tester inserted in the center comes out clean. Cool on a wire rack and refrigerate an hour before eating. The mini pies can be frozen and enjoyed later.

Nutrition Facts for Mini Pumpkin Pies

Ingredients	Calories	Sodium	Carbs	Fiber	Protein
Graham Cracker Crumbs	390	630	69	3	6
Granulated Sugar	45	0	12	0	0
Salted Butter	408	328	0	0	0
Pumpkin	135	15	30	9	3
Large Eggs	148	140	0	0	13
Granulated Sugar	258	0	66	0	0
Dark Brown Sugar	90	0	24	0	0
Half and Half	160	48	5	0	4
Totals:	1634	1161	206	12	26
1 Pumpkin Pie	**136**	**97**	**21**	**2**	**2**

****

Rhubarb Crumble
Makes Ten (½-cup servings)

Ingredients
1½ pounds rhubarb stalks, cut into ½-inch pieces
¾ cup granulated sugar
2 tablespoons cornstarch
1 teaspoon cinnamon
¼ teaspoon cardamom
½ cup whole wheat flour
¼ cup walnuts, chopped
2 tablespoons light brown sugar, firmly packed
½ teaspoon cinnamon
4 tablespoons salted butter, cold

Preheat the oven to 375°F. Grease a 2-quart baking dish. Cut the rhubarb stalks into ½-inch diced pieces. Place them in a medium bowl with the sugar, cornstarch, cinnamon, and cardamom. Mix thoroughly and place the rhubarb mixture on the bottom of the prepared dish.

For the topping, combine the flour, walnuts, brown sugar, and cinnamon in a medium bowl. Cut the butter in with a pastry cutter until the topping is crumbly. Sprinkle the topping over the rhubarb layer, leaving some areas where the mixture shows through.

Bake for 40 to 45 minutes or until hot and bubbling. Serve warm or cold. It can be frozen in one half-cup portions and thawed out later.

Nutrition Facts for Rhubarb Crumble

Ingredients	Calories	Sodium	Carbs	Fiber	Protein
Rhubarb	147	35	39	15	8
Granulated Sugar	581	0	150	0	0
Cornstarch	60	0	14	0	0
Whole Wheat Flour	200	0	42	6	8
Walnuts	200	0	4	2	5
Light Brown Suger	90	0	24	0	0
Salted Butter	408	0	0	0	0
Totals:	1686	35	273	23	21

Rhubarb Crumble (½ cup)	**169**	**3.5**	**27**	**2**	**2**

****

Strawberry Shortcakes
Makes Ten

Ingredients

 1 cup all-purpose flour
 ¾ cup whole wheat flour
 2 tablespoons granulated sugar
 1 teaspoon baking powder
 ½ teaspoon baking soda
 4 tablespoons salted butter, cold
  5.3 ounces Dannon, Light & Fit, Strawberry Greek yogurt
  1 large egg, lightly beaten
  3 tablespoons half-and-half
  1 teaspoon vanilla extract
   2 cups strawberries, sliced
   2 tablespoons granulated sugar
    whipped topping

Preheat the oven to 350°F. Line a cookie sheet with parchment paper. In a large bowl, mix together the flours, sugar, baking powder, and baking soda. Cut in the butter until the mixture resembles coarse cornmeal.

Add the yogurt, beaten egg, half and half, and vanilla extract, all at once. Stir with a fork until just blended. Gently knead with additional flour until it adheres together. It should be slightly tacky but not wet.

Form the dough into ten rounds about 1 inch high. Transfer them to the prepared cookie sheet. Bake for 16 to 20 minutes or until a cake tester comes out clean. Cool on a wire rack.

Prepare the filling while the shortcakes are cooling by placing the sliced strawberries in a small bowl with the added sugar. When cool, cut the shortcakes horizontally and fill them with the strawberry mixture and your favorite whipped topping. (The whipped cream topping nutrition facts are not included in the shortcake totals.) Uncut shortcakes can be frozen and eaten later.

Nutrition Facts for Strawberry Shortcakes

Ingredients	Calories	Sodium	Carbs	Fiber	Protein
All-Purpose Flour	440	0	92	2	12
Whole Wheat Flour	300	0	63	9	12
Granulated Sugar	90	0	24	0	0
Salted Butter	510	410	0	0	1
Strawberry Greek Yogurt	80	45	9	1	12
Large Egg	74	70	0	0	6
Half and Half	60	18	2	0	1
Vanilla Extract	12	0	0	0	0
Strawberries	106	4	25	7	2
Granulated Sugar	90	0	24	0	0
Totals:	1762	547	239	19	46

	Calories	Sodium	Carbs	Fiber	Protein
1 Strawberry Shortcake	176	54	23	2	5
Without Straw/Sugar	156	54	19	1	4.5

Copyright Acknowledgments

Celebration
Words and Music by Robert Earl Bell, Ronald Bell, George Brown, Robert Spike Mickens, Claydes Smith, James Taylor, Dennis Thomas, and Earl Toon.
© 1980 Old River Music and Primary Wave 3 Songs
All Rights Administered by Warner Tamerlane Publishing Corp.
All Rights Reserved
Used by Permission
Reprinted by Permission of Hal Leonard LLC
Pages 11-12

Cold as Ice
Words and Music by Louis Grammatico and Michael Jones
© 1977 Somerset Sings Publishing Inc.
All Rights Administered by Warner Chappell Music Corp.
All Rights Reserved
Used by Permission
Reprinted by Permission of Hal Leonard LLC
Pages 25-26

Dreams
Words and Music by Stevie Nicks
© 1976 Kobalt Songs Music Publishing
Administered by Kobalt Music Publishing Inc.
All Rights Reserved
International Copyright Secured
Used by Permission
Reprinted by Permission of Hal Leonard LLC
Pages 44-45

Fly Like an Eagle
Words and Music by Steve Miller
© 1976 by Sailor Music
Copyright Renewed
All Rights Reserved
Used by Permission

Reprinted by Permission of Hal Leonard LLC
Pages 98-99

Food, Glorious Food
Words and Music by Lionel Bart
from the Broadway Musical, OLIVER
© 1960 Lakeview Music Publishing Co. LTD,
Hollis Music, and Tro Essex Music Group
Copyright Renewed
All Rights Reserved
International Copyright Secured
Used by Permission
Reprinted by Permission of Hal Leonard LLC
Pages 21-22

From Russia With Love
Words and Music by John Barry and Lionel Bart
© 1963 (Renewed) EMI Unart Catalog Inc.
All Rights Administered by Sony Music Publishing (US) LLC,
8 Music Square West
Nashville, TN 37203-3204
All Rights Reserved
Used by Permission
Reprinted by Permission of Hal Leonard LLC
Pages 71-72

Helplessly Hoping
Words & Music by Stephen Stills
Copyright © 1969 Stay Straight Music, Gold Hill Music, Inc.,
and Icebag Music Corp.
Copyright Renewed
All Rights for Stay Straight Music Administered by BMG Rights
Management (US) LLC
All Rights for Gold Hill Music, Inc. and Icebag Music Corp.
Administered by Wixen Music Publishing, Inc.
All Rights Reserved

Undun

We May Never Pass This Way Again